Abigail Gordon loves to write about the fascinating combination of medicine and romance from her home in a Cheshire village. She is active in local affairs, and is even called upon to write the script for the annual village pantomime! Her eldest son is a hospital manager, and helps with all her medical research. As part of a close-knit family, she treasures having two of her sons living close by and the third one not too far away. This also gives her the added pleasure of being able to watch her delightful grandchildren growing up.

Also by Abigail Gordon

Christmas Magic in Heatherdale
Heatherdale's Shy Nurse
A Father for Poppy
His Christmas Bride-to-Be

The Doctors of Swallowbrook Farm miniseries

Swallowbrook's Winter Bride
Spring Proposal in Swallowbrook
Marriage Miracle in Swallowbrook
Swallowbrook's Wedding of the Year

Discover more at millsandboon.co.uk.

THE SHY NURSE'S CHRISTMAS WISH

ABIGAIL GORDON

MILLS & BOON

Published in Great Britain 2018
by Mills & Boon, an imprint of HarperCollins*Publishers*
1 London Bridge Street, London, SE1 9GF

ISBN: 978-0-263-07708-7

MIX
Paper from
responsible sources
FSC C007454

This book is produced from independently certified FSC™ paper
to ensure responsible forest management.
For more information visit www.harpercollins.co.uk/green.

Printed and bound in Great Britain
by CPI Group (UK) Ltd, Croydon, CR0 4YY

CHAPTER ONE

THE TRAIN WAS already at the platform when Darcey Howard got to the station. As she heaved her case on board she saw at a glance that it was crowded and about to leave at any moment. Tired and harassed after the happenings of the last few days, she felt like weeping.

Under other circumstances she would have booked a seat for the journey, wanting to arrive at her destination cool and collected with an air of quiet competence about her, but instead she was overwrought and going to be standing all the way there from the looks of it as there were no empty seats to be seen at a glance.

Until a man nearby looked up from the laptop on the table in front of him and, on seeing her standing in the doorway of the carriage, moved a pile of paperwork off the seat opposite him. Pointing to it, he lifted her luggage onto the rack provided while she sank down gratefully into the empty space with a whispered word of thanks and her head bent, her gaze fixed unseeingly on the floor beneath her feet.

When he'd seated himself again Daniel Osbourne observed her briefly.

While hoisting her case he'd seen the name of the town that she was heading for and it was the same as where he lived, which was a coincidence, but he had no time to chatter about that sort of thing.

Having been away on a seminar about new treatments in the orthopaedic field he had been making copious notes about what he had seen and heard while there, and having found a seat for the pale-looking person now seated opposite, he was in no mood to talk.

Yet he couldn't help wondering what was taking her to Seahaven where he lived and worked. Was it its coastal attractiveness, its pleasant town, or like many folk a need for treatment in Oceans House with problems of the body that could make movement an ordeal in one form or another.

He was employed as top surgeon at the place and having been away for two weeks was looking forward to a restful evening with those he loved before going back to his usual work tomorrow.

It had been Alexander, Darcey Howard's eighteen-year-old brother, who had wiped out the pleasure of receiving the news that she had been accepted as a ward sister at Oceans House.

There was just the two of them, brother and sister, having been left parentless some years ago, and since then Darcey, as the eldest, had cared for Alex like the mother he had lost, while at the same time studying for a degree in orthopaedics at a nearby medical college and commuting daily from the home that they shared.

On getting her degree in nursing she had worked on the orthopaedic wards of a local hospital with reasonable contentment until seeing a vacancy for a ward sister in the beautiful coastal town of Seahaven, with accommodation available in the apartment complex at the side of the hospital building.

It had meant a move to new surroundings, living in a new environment, and she'd been happy that Alex had shown no reluctance to move there with her as he was only eighteen and keen to follow in her footsteps by studying for a degree similar to her own.

In fact, he'd been quite excited about the move at first until one night he had talked non-stop about two of his friends who were taking a year out after high school, wanting to see the world first, and had invited him to join them, much to Darcey's dismay.

She had listened painfully to the way that Alexander had put to one side as if they had never existed the long years that she had cared for him lovingly after losing their parents in an avalanche while on a skiing holiday. Darcey had always accepted that one day Alex would want to leave the safe cocoon she had made for him, but not so soon, she'd thought achingly.

At university he would be where she could see him, care for him still from a distance, whereas if he was travelling the world he could be swallowed up for ever, she'd thought, and it had hurt to know how easy it was for Alex to find freedom from life's burdens as if he had more exciting things to do, when she Darcey had given up so much over the years.

It was the first time since losing their parents that they'd had a disagreement, as Darcey, ten years older than her brother, had always been there for Alex no matter what. Comforting him when he'd cried for his mother, carefully budgeting what money they'd had, making sure Alex had everything he needed.

She had known that one day he would break free from the bonds of her love and been quite happy with the thought, but not now, as what he was planning had thrown her into confusion and deep dismay.

When she'd expressed her hurt at his change of plan, Alexander had been difficult and unapproachable, and their quarrel had made her contemplate turning down her new job. But, hurt by Alex's attitude, she decided to put herself first for once in her life, and now, tired and dejected, was travelling towards the new life she had chosen for herself in spite of the anxiety that was consuming her on his behalf, while he was involved in last-minute preparations before he and his two companions flew out to lands far away, from where he had promised faithfully to keep in touch.

He had promised to be at the railway station to see her off earlier but hadn't kept to the arrangement. Hence her late boarding of the train where she would have been standing if it hadn't been for the man opposite who had now returned to his laptop after his brief but welcome assistance, and seemed to have no wish to be involved further, for which she was thankful. Darcey was glad that the seating arrangement was for just two passengers instead of the usual four, and also the fact that she could hear the refreshments trolley trundling along the carriage.

She was more than ready for a drink and a bite and when the trolley stopped beside them, and in a mad moment she asked him if he would like a coffee or something similar as a token of her gratitude for his assistance on the crowded train.

'No, thanks just the same,' he said briskly, taking his glance off the laptop for a moment. 'Just see to yourself and if I may be allowed to say so you look as if some light refreshment is needed to combat exhaustion.' With that he turned back to what he'd been doing, leaving her to squirm at the thought of what she must look like.

She knew that her hair, a soft honey gold, looked lifeless, and many sleepless nights had left lines beneath eyes wide and blue. She'd lost weight and felt bony rather than slender, and a quick sideways glance in his direction, tanned and supple-looking with hair dark and waving, and deep hazel eyes, did nothing to raise her spirits.

As the train picked up speed, her thoughts returned to Alexander, and how his travelling companions seemed decent enough, but she still couldn't help worrying about their safety, being so far away. She would have liked to have been there when their flight left but there had been a change of plan by the three of them, causing a delay that might have meant a late arrival for her new position in hospital care. Feeling that she had endured enough misery over recent days, Darcey had decided to keep to her original arrangements for travelling to Oceans House.

She groaned softly and the man opposite observed her before asking, 'Are you all right? Not in pain, physical or mental?'

'No. I'm fine, thanks,' she said, perking up to avoid any further questioning from a stranger, and turned her thoughts to the apartment that was going to be her home from now on, and some of the excitement that had been there before Alex had decided to branch out on his own came back.

An announcement over the loudspeaker system broke into her thoughts, informing travellers that the main station on the line, and her destination, was the next stop. She rose to her feet at the same time as the stranger who had taken pity on her, and as he reached her case down effortlessly from the rack above and placed it beside her she was hoping that she might be seeing the last of him, as it was clear that he had her listed as a helpless creature, not that she could blame him.

He was closing the laptop and shrugging into an expensive winter jacket, ready for off, and Darcey wondered what he did for a living, and decided that if there was a taxi queue at the station she was going to join it with all speed to avoid further assistance from him.

There was a queue, a long one, but the man from the train didn't move towards it because someone had come to meet him. He was getting into a smart car parked a few feet away and Darcey saw him lean over and plant a kiss on the cheek of the attractive woman in the driving seat before it pulled away onto the road in the winter afternoon, and she thought wistfully that he looked like someone who had it made from all angles.

'So, Cordelia, what has it been like with me away and you landed with the brood at the Young Sailors' Club?' Daniel Osbourne was asking quizzically of his sister, who had turned out to chauffeur him home, when he caught a glimpse of the woman who'd piqued his interest on the train and wondered if she would be able to find her way to where she was going if she hadn't visited the place before.

Yet he thought he'd done quite a bit of fussing during the rail journey, so enough was enough, and, as Cordelia pulled out into the moving traffic homeward bound, he thought the odds were that the woman, whoever she was, would have seen enough of him and neither needed nor wanted any more assistance.

He'd had no doubts about her lowness of spirit from the moment of helping her with her case, and if he hadn't been so engrossed with the paperwork from the course that he'd just been on he might have done more.

'The "brood", as you describe them, have been in trouble,' Cordelia told him with an affectionate glance at the man beside her. 'They have missed you, of course, two of them especially who have ended up in Oceans House with fractures and suchlike that A and E passed on because they were too complex for them to treat.

'But I hope that you're not going anywhere near the place tonight because we're having friends round for supper and we want you with us if you're not too stressed after being away over the last fortnight. We're letting the children stay up as the moment your name was mentioned the girls were keen to see you. So what do you say?' she questioned.

His expression was sombre after the news about what the sailing club had been up to and he commented, 'There are other doctors at Oceans House as well as me who will take good care of the injured miscreants.' Now he was smiling. 'And with regard to the invitation to supper I say, yes, of course. I've got something for the children in my luggage and if they get tired I'll tell them a bedtime story. You know how much I love your daughters.'

'Yes, I do,' she told him wistfully. 'I wish you had a family of your own, though.'

'Don't fret about me,' was the reply. 'At the time when I could have done something about it I was dumb about a lot of things, blinkered by my own concerns, such as getting my degree and providing for us both as Katrina had expensive tastes and a short fuse. She thought herself right in all things and since I divorced her I haven't seen her—which suits me fine.

'But you know all about that don't you, sis?' he questioned as Cordelia stopped the car outside a block of apartments with sea views, not too far from Oceans House and near to where she lived contentedly with her husband and two small girls who adored their Uncle Daniel.

'Yes, of course I remember,' she said gently. 'Maybe one day you'll—'

'Don't ever be too hopeful about that,' he said dryly. 'I'm content to give my time to my patients and when called upon take my place in the lifeboat. Plus getting to know the young teens in the sailing club and helping them learn how to handle the rescue safety boat. But some of them need a firm hand, and with regard to supper I shall look forward to being with you and yours once I've showered and changed.'

'Good,' Cordelia enthused. 'I wasn't sure if a gruelling fortnight away might have wearied you too much.'

'Not at all,' he assured her, with the thought unspoken that he'd also had a cheerless return rail journey on a packed train. That brought to mind again the memory of the fellow passenger that he'd taken under his wing, and he ended up with the feeling that he'd been bossy and interfering. Hopefully they wouldn't meet again.

Spending time with Cordelia and Lawrence's children was always a pleasure. Aged seven and five years, the two small girls always greeted Daniel with delight and excitement because he never arrived empty-handed, and that evening was no different.

But the memory of his conversation with their mother in the car on the way home from the rail station was lingering, and he asked himself, as he sometimes did, why he had committed himself to living alone when it would be so easy to respond to the interest that women frequently showed in him. But having made one mistake, he would never be in a hurry to make another.

Darcey had arrived at Oceans House and, having obtained the key to the small apartment allocated to her, was taking stock of the premises that, circumstances permitting, were going to be her home for some time to come.

It contained a bedroom, a shower and a cosy enough sitting room with a through kitchen adjoining. As she took off her jacket and sank down wearily onto the nearest chair the thought was there of how happy she would have been if the original arrangements that she and Alex had made regarding both their futures had stood firm.

There would have been none of the anxiety on her part because before he had developed a yearning to see the world he had been accepted at university, and been offered accommodation in the halls of residence there, which would have meant that they could have seen each other regularly. It was the kind of situation that did happen and usually parents would be involved, but theirs, hers and Alexander's, were long gone. She knew that if she didn't calm down, her own future was going to be threatened and then what would she have left?

For a crazy moment the memory of the man in the train came back, with his calm authoritarian manner and casual concern about her well-being. She could imagine him having an attractive wife and family waiting eagerly for his return to an orderly organised life while her own was a shambles, but why concern herself about that when she was never likely to be in his company again?

Her phone rang at that moment and as she fished it out of her hand luggage, Darcey prayed it was Alex. They'd barely been on speaking terms when she'd left and that had hurt the most of all. If he had just turned up at the rail station for a few moments it would have been a move towards peace between them. But there hadn't been any sign of him and she'd waited until the guard had blown the whistle to announce the train was about to depart before she'd hurriedly boarded the train, and felt like weeping when she'd discovered how little room there had been for last-minute arrivals. But someone had seen her plight and she had been less than grateful for his assistance, which was awful, she thought as the phone continued to ring.

It was not Alex who spoke when she answered. The voice in her ear was that of the overseer of the pleasant small property that she and her younger brother had just vacated, who was phoning to thank her for promptly settling all rent owing to his firm, and wishing her everything that was good for the future.

With regard to her signing the necessary forms regarding her residence in the hospital property, Darcey had been given all the details of procedure on her arrival there and been informed that the staff restaurant was open until late if she wanted a meal. As she fought back tears at the kind thought from her ex-landlord, hunger was rising. The last time she'd eaten had been from the refreshment trolley on the train, and after food she needed sleep if she was to appear on the wards the next morning with her wits about her, she told herself. But whether sleep would come to her as easily as the food she sought was another matter.

As Cordelia watched her brother play with her daughters that evening, their conversation of the afternoon came back to trouble her. Was Daniel really so disinterested in a family life of his own? she wondered. A couple of her friends were present and would be there in a flash if he should show interest. Both were recently divorced and ready to try again.

But that was the difference, she thought, he wasn't. He'd made one mistake along those lines, having married the wrong woman in the petulant Katrina and was not going to make another. Yet watching him with Bethany and Katie, his small nieces, it was clear to see that he would make an excellent father to children of his own given the chance.

He went once the children were in bed and on the point of leaving told his hosts, 'I won't be seeing much of you next week. I'm in Theatre most of the time and there are going to be some staff changes due to retirement and pregnancies, so I will be hoping for no high tides.'

As Darcey was drifting off to sleep the phone call that she'd yearned for came through, with Alexander sounding awkward and apologetic, asking if she was all right, and after assuring him that she was she enquired the same of him, and was told breezily that everything was great and he would phone her again soon.

The brief conversation hadn't been exactly heartwarming but after he'd gone off the line she was too tired to think any further than at least he'd been in touch, and that tomorrow she would be starting her new life in Seahaven, which meant that she was going to have to improve her appearance after today's stresses. After that exhaustion claimed her.

She was awakened in the middle of the night by the sound of an ambulance somewhere nearby, with sirens breaking into the silence, and for a moment she was confused by the strangeness of her new surroundings, but as she gazed around the place that was to be her home for as long as she was employed at Oceans House it wasn't hard to work out that the staff accommodation where she was going to be based was the nearest building to Emergency.

As senior doctor at the place, Daniel Osbourne often did his ward rounds late in the morning depending on how much time he had spent in Theatre first thing, planned or unexpected as the case may be, so it was almost midday when he came into the main children's ward with a couple of registrars in tow to check on the progress of those he had already treated or were awaiting their turn.

On observing a different ward sister, pristine in a new uniform and immaculately turned out, with golden hair tied back from a face that was familiar from the day before, Daniel pondered if this could really be the tired and listless traveller he had taken under his wing and thought, Surely not!

The woman had been moving from bed to bed when he appeared, giving medication and taking temperatures, while members of her staff dealt with other duties allocated to them with regard to child patient care, but on hearing his voice she became still and turned slowly to meet his gaze.

Darcey had known it was the man from the train by the brisk and authoritative tone, and aware that she would be expected to accompany him on his round she went to stand beside him and introduced herself, praying that in a short space of time, namely the matter of hours that she had been on the ward, she would have remembered correctly the answers to any questions that he might have for her with regard to the young patients there.

But to her surprise what he had to say first referred to herself as he queried, 'Why didn't you say that you were coming here to work when we were on the train?'

'I had no need to, or so I thought,' she protested faintly. 'And I was so tired.'

'But of course you were,' he agreed crisply. He glanced at the two registrars, who were chatting to a girl on the nearest bed with one of her legs in traction. 'So, shall we proceed, Sister?'

'Yes, Mr Osbourne,' she said meekly, and as his companions wasted no time in joining them she smiled at the girl who'd had their attention and told him, 'Olivia seems to be resigned to her plight for the moment and I'm told that when some of her school friends appear each day in the late afternoon there is a lot of chatter and news, which helps to get the hours over for her somewhat.'

'Mmm… I'm sure that it must,' he murmured, his attention on the young patient and the state of her leg, which was supported by attachments from an overhead frame. Turning to Darcey, he said, 'The fracture of the tibia occurred during a hockey match and this is the result, the leg immobilised until healing of the bone is achieved. Have you dealt with this kind of thing before?'

'Yes, a few times,' she told him, thinking that her appearance of the day before hadn't been one to instil confidence, but surely it might now. As they moved on to the next bed she went on to say, 'I have trained and worked in orthopaedics ever since it became my specialist subject at university, and the opportunity to work in a hospital in a beautiful coastal area was too tempting to pass by.' With a sigh, she added, 'I wasn't expecting to be alone in my change of scene but far countries seem to have got in the way of my plans, and, as you saw on the train yesterday, I was at a low ebb.'

'Mmm, so it appeared,' he commented, without showing much interest, and moved towards the next bed, followed by Darcey and the two registrars.

It was over. He had done the rounds and was about to depart, and his thoroughness had been no surprise to her, with his keen observations of the slightest thing that had caught his eye, whether it be good or not so good.

Once he had left there was a buzz of conversation amongst the nurses that was centred on Daniel Osbourne and all of it was complimentary so that she was left with no doubt regarding his popularity in spite of his no-nonsense approach.

With regard to herself, Darcey was cringing at the way she'd been so free and easy with her comments that might have given him the impression that it was a failed romance she'd been hinting at when it had been far from that.

When her lunch break came round, instead of making her way to the staff restaurant, Darcey went out into the cold air of the seaside promenade that went past the hospital and stood gazing out to where a choppy blue sea rose and fell in the distance.

As she turned to go back into the warmth of the hospital a smart black car pulled up beside her at the pavement edge and he was there again, the down-to-earth doctor who seemed to be everywhere she turned. Winding the car window down, he asked what she was doing out there in the cold without a jacket.

'It is the first time I've been able to see the sea since I came,' she told him. 'When I arrived last night it was dark, and the same this morning when I reported to the ward, and I've only been out here a moment.'

Daniel was smiling and she thought that he was different away from his duties at the hospital and looking after lost souls like herself on the train, but he was right, the cold was biting and she was hungry. What did he do about lunch? she thought. Had he already eaten? He was pulling away from the kerb, giving her no time to ask, and she went inside with hunger calling and curiosity taking hold. Where did he live? she wondered, and with who, and was that his day finished?

* * *

It was not, by far. Daniel was about to make a brief visit to the sailing club that he had arranged for teens with time on their hands. He usually put in an appearance in the evening but having been away, and remembering his sister's comments of the night before, he was keen to see the state of things at the place and what he observed there didn't please him.

His helper with the running of the club was an old guy called Ely, a retired fisherman who was usually to be found on the premises, but not today it seemed, and the boat that was the magnet that brought young folks to the club was in a state of repair in the harbour.

What had been going on? he pondered. When he called at Ely's cottage nearby to get up to date with the situation, his wife Bridget told him that her husband was in hospital with a heart problem, where he had been when the boat had been damaged.

'With you both not around, the would-be sailors were impatient to be out there and they took the boat without permission,' she told him, 'and came unstuck on a rocky reef, which meant the lifeboat having to turn out. Two of the lads were injured and are in Oceans House.' With that cheerful item of news to digest Daniel returned to the hospital to carry on bringing mobility to the immobile in one form or another for the rest of the day, and if Darcey had still questioned his movements after watching him drive away in the lunch hour she would have had her answer on seeing him moving purposefully along the main hospital corridor in the direction of the operating theatre in the early afternoon.

In the evening that followed, Darcey was restless. There had been no more phone calls from Alexander, no contentment at the end of her first day at Oceans House, nothing to brighten the last hours of it. Just a mediocre night of entertainment on the television screen in the small apartment that was now her home. Her time on the ward had been great, she thought, but what now?

On impulse she reached for the warm winter jacket that she'd travelled in and her knee-high boots and without another thought went out into the dark night where a moon hung over the sea that was less choppy than earlier in the day.

The promenade was well lit with a selection of bars and restaurants to choose from, but Darcey was not entranced at the thought of dining alone in a strange place where she didn't know anyone, and when she came to the teenage meeting place at the far end of the promenade that, unknown to her, was Daniel Osbourne's project she paused outside the wooden building and looked around her with interest.

Nearby was the harbour and she saw a roomy boat there in the process of being repaired, and as she looked around her she heard the sound of young voices on the night air. A short distance away was the lifeboat house, shuttered and locked until needed, and as she lingered curiously a deeper voice that was becoming familiar caught her attention as it spoke with authority into what had become silence inside the wooden building and she was rooted to the spot.

When Daniel Osbourne had finished speaking the young members of the organisation came pouring out as the clock on a nearby church tower hit the stroke of ten, and having no desire to be seen hovering outside the place she quickly hurried through the crowd of teenagers as they spread out over the promenade, breathing a sigh of relief when the staff accommodation for Ocean House came into sight. Thank goodness he hadn't seen her lurking outside while he'd been speaking to the young people.

Daniel thought whimsically that the new sister had had no cause to flee from his presence. She'd been unaware that he had been on foot amongst the kids, and short of sprinting after her in the early dark of an October night had to be satisfied with just quickening his pace. But the apartments had come into view and she'd been inside in a flash with the door locked behind her.

It was just a matter of common courtesy to make sure that a newcomer amongst those he worked with was home safely after wandering alone amongst the night crowds who drank in the bars and ate in the restaurants on the promenade, and with that thought in mind he proceeded to his own residence, which wasn't far away, where he lived in solitary comfort that was edged with loneliness.

After her speedy return to base Darcey made a hot drink and pondered on the moments that she'd spent outside the place where Daniel Osbourne and the teenagers had been meeting. He hadn't sounded pleased about something and had been making it known, she thought. The young folk had seemed chastened when they'd come filing out into the dark night.

'Young Sailors' Club' was what it had said above the door of the wooden building at the end of the promenade and next to it had been the harbour where the boat was being repaired. So was it something to do with that to blame for bringing forth his annoyance?

Daniel could have told her that it was. He had started the club to keep the kids occupied and off the streets by training them in the complexities of sailing in the rescue safety boat, which was a smaller craft than the lifeboat but just as necessary in moments of danger nearer to the shore. No members were allowed to take it away from its moorings without himself or Ely being there.

But with the old guy hospitalised and Daniel absent, some of the teenagers left to their own devices had taken it out and damaged it against a rocky outcrop. So much so that the lifeboat had been called out to get them all safely back on shore, which, as far as Daniel was concerned, was an even greater annoyance as it could have been avoided if they hadn't broken the rules.

Two of the young guys had been injured in the mishap and when his sister had informed him on his return that they were in Oceans House with fractures, his annoyance had been normal, but it had peaked when he'd seen the boat.

Hence the stern reprimand to the rest that Darcey must have heard through the open doors of their meeting place, and it hadn't improved his mood as he'd been bringing the evening to a close when he'd caught a glimpse of her through the open door on the pavement outside, alone in the winter night, which had brought forth his effort to catch her up as she'd hurried back to her own place.

And what now he thought with mild irony as he settled down in front of the fire in the sitting room of the tasteful apartment that had long been his residence.

Tonight would have been another example of him interfering in the life of the new sister on the children's ward if he'd caught her up. What was the matter with him?

If she'd seen him sprinting along behind her down the promenade she would have thought him insane when he had merely been trying to be helpful, but that was it. From now on he would keep a low profile where she was concerned. His only contact would be at the bedsides of their young patients.

CHAPTER TWO

UNAWARE OF THE promise that Daniel had made to himself the night before, when he had finished his ward round the next day and was about to depart Darcey said, 'I am so sorry about your boat, Dr Osbourne, and I do hope that the two boys who are being treated here will soon recover. I was on the promenade last night near the harbour and saw it.' She added with a wistfulness that surprised him, 'If my young brother lived here, he would be most keen to join your sailing club.'

'So he doesn't live near, then?' he commented with the chaos of the night before still upon him.

'No. I'm afraid not,' she replied, and when a small child in one of the cots began to cry she went to him and lifting him carefully, soothed the little boy gently until he was comforted, and watching her Daniel thought that whoever had designated her to be sister-in-charge of the children's ward had got it right.

On the point of departure, he informed her, 'Needless to say, I've seen the two lads with the injuries and am treating them myself now that I'm back. We are talking about a badly fractured leg and a spinal problem at the moment, and tonight I intend to visit my old friend Ely who is in a hospital in the town centre with a heart problem and doesn't know about the boat and the sea rescue.'

His wife has sensibly kept it from him under the circumstances. As there was never really any time for chatting in his working day he turned to go, yet it didn't stop him from turning for a last look at her with the child in her arms.

The day had run its course. The night staff had arrived and Darcey and those she worked with were homeward bound. She had been the last to leave as she'd needed to discuss problems with the night sister that had arisen with one of their young patients just before the changeover, and when she left the ward the corridor outside was empty apart from a small group gathered near the exit consisting of Daniel Osbourne, the attractive woman who had been waiting for him in the car at the station, and two small girls who were cuddling up to him.

If there had been another exit close by she would have taken it, but there wasn't, and hastening past the small family group she was out in the cold winter night in a flash, her curiosity about his background satisfied after seeing the happy family group.

As Darcey walked the short distance to her apartment loneliness was wrapping itself around her. It was something that she'd only experienced since

Alex had gone, and having just seen the happy family group in the corridor it had hit her even more as she thought that she had been right in her surmise that Daniel Osbourne would have an attractive wife and adorable children, and didn't begrudge him them. He was too charismatic and attractive not to have a family of his own.

Engrossed with his visitors, he hadn't seen her coming swiftly towards them and by the time it registered she was past and going through the outer doors of the hospital into the night. As he gazed after her Daniel was conscious of her solitariness and hoped that there was someone else in Sister Darcey Howard's life besides the unavailable young brother that she'd mentioned.

Cordelia and the children had been on their way home from the birthday party of one of their friends and as they'd had to pass the hospital she had taken them to see him briefly. When the passer-by had disappeared she asked, 'Who was that, Daniel?'

'The day sister in charge of the children's ward,' he replied briefly, and volunteered no further information because he had none, and once those he loved had said goodbye he didn't wait long before calling it a day and returning to the familiar solitude of his apartment, which usually replaced the day's strains and stresses with tranquillity, but not this time. He was restless, couldn't settle, but wouldn't admit to himself that it had anything to do with having watched Darcey leave without any assurance that once she had taken off the garments of her profession she wouldn't be exploring the night life of the promenade on her own, as she had done the night before.

Daniel was not to know there was nothing further from Darcey's mind. She was feeling low and lost, and after a snack followed by a shower Darcey went to bed and until drowsiness took her into sleep, she spent the time listening in vain for the phone to ring.

A fourth day had dawned with no more contact from Alex and as the three young men were staying anywhere they could with friends and relatives until flight time she was wishing she had been more adamant about him keeping in touch. But something new was appearing in her life as well as his. Alex was happy in the choices he was making, so why shouldn't she be the same?

The opportunity was there that hadn't been present before for her to experience something new in the form of a freedom of her own after all the years that she had cared so devotedly for her young brother. She had put him first in everything and suddenly that was no more, the need for it was gone.

But she still had to know that all was well with him before even contemplating anything else, and, as if he'd read her mind, just as she was about to go to present herself on the ward, Alex called. He told her that he hoped that she would be happy in her new job and that he would keep in touch when he could.

To hear his voice was solace after the hours of anxiety that he had caused her.

Over recent days the smile with which the new ward sister greeted Daniel and his entourage on their arrival on the ward had been missing, but he saw that today there was a change, not totally but she was more relaxed, less pale and stressed than of late. When he stopped at the first bed in the ward, where its little occupant's condition was causing concern, Darcey was as clear and confident as she always was when doing the rounds with him and was tuned in immediately to his comments, just the same as while he was examining the young girl who had suffered a spinal injury after falling off a swing the previous day and was in much pain.

At that moment the child was in a fretful doze, unaware that she was the centre of attention. Daniel read the notes clipped to the bottom of the bed and said, 'Sister, I want this child to have a scan and some blood tests to check if there is some injury that hasn't shown itself previously and has surfaced during the night.'

'Yes, Mr Osbourne,' she said levelly, and immediately sent for a porter to follow his instructions. Then, picking up her desk phone, she rang the parents of the injured child to explain there was a new development regarding their daughter's accident, which came as a shock as they had been at her bedside until late the previous evening and had only left when she had fallen into a deep sleep that had indicated no cause for alarm.

But the little girl had awakened in a winter dawn feverish and in pain, and as the porter moved swiftly towards the ultrasound unit with the crying child on the trolley Daniel was close behind, having left his second-in-command to do the rest of the rounds in the children's ward.

The doctor's name was Brendan Stokes and Darcey braced herself to spend the next hour or so being patronised by him. He had already asked her for a date and been refused because he was arrogant and pushy, and it annoyed her that on something as important as caring for sick children he was still eyeing her up and down. While Daniel Osbourne was just the opposite, this one was the opportunist of all time, she thought.

But having seen the man on her mind in the corridor with his family the other day, it was easy to understand his contentment. With a wife and children of such a kind he must be totally happy. His interest in her would be merely keeping an eye on a newcomer to Oceans House, and as far as she was concerned looking after Alex all those years had left little time to make any commitments with the opposite sex.

There had been a couple of times in the past that she'd let herself be dated by local Romeos, but always Alexander had been her main concern, which had put a dampener on every occasion.

When Daniel came back, she observed him questioningly and he said with reasonable calm, 'I was concerned that we might have missed something when the child was brought in, but there is nothing of that nature. It seems that she was in the process of developing a chest infection at the time of the accident and now it is making itself felt and causing her temperature to soar. Our young patient is on her way back to bed and I've put her on antibiotics to cope with it. So keep a close watch on her, Sister, and don't hesitate to send for me if you have any more concerns about her.'

'Yes, of course,' she replied, 'and I'll make sure that the night staff are fully informed.'

He was looking around him and questioned, 'Where is Dr Stokes? Has he done the rounds?'

'Not quite,' she told him, pointing to a small side ward off the main one.

'Right,' he replied. 'I'll join him,' and as he turned to go, 'Is all well with you?'

'Ye-es,' she said hesitatingly, and he glanced at her.

'Are you sure? I've thought that you seemed to have lost some of your zest. The kind of work that the likes of us have to cope with can be wearing sometimes, to say the least.'

His concern was quickening her heartbeat and her colour was rising as she repeated that she was fine. Partly reassured, he left her and went to find his assistant and with his departure Darcey wondered what Daniel Osbourne would have said if she'd told him the reason for the melancholy in her that he had picked up on. He would probably have thought she was crazy to be so upset at the freedom that Alexander's departure had given her.

When a couple of the nurses said they were going to go for a meal at a nearby restaurant on the promenade when they'd finished for the day and did she want to join them, she said yes, and thought that if Daniel saw her out and about he would have no cause to question her lowness of spirit.

Inevitably his name came up in the conversation during the meal as the three nurses chatted about their working day, and Darcey commented that it was to be hoped that the sailing club he was connected with didn't meet every night or he wouldn't have much time to spend with his family if both his days and nights were spoken for all the time.

The comment caused her two companions to observe her in surprise and they wasted no time in informing her that Dr Osbourne wasn't married, that he was a free agent, and if he ever decided to change that situation there would be no shortage of would-be brides.

'It would have been his sister and her children that you saw him with,' they told her, and Darcey listened in amazement. 'The dishy doctor was married way back, but it didn't work out, from all accounts, and it seems that since then he has steered clear of matrimony with all its joys and sorrows, and gives all his attention to his sister's children. You'll know from seeing him on the wards how good he is with young ones.'

'Er...yes,' she agreed weakly, and thanked the unseen fates that had prevented her from saying anything out of turn to him. She'd been crazy to take it for granted that he was a family man that day, that the woman and children were his, and wondered what it was that had been the cause of his marriage break-up.

It was still early evening when Darcey arrived back at the apartment after the meal with the two nurses, and now, thinking back, it seemed a long time since her brief conversation with Daniel Osbourne after they'd done the ward rounds, but short as it had been there had been a oneness about it that had never been present before with any man she'd met.

The man on her mind had gone straight to the harbour after leaving Oceans House Hospital at the end of the day to enquire what progress the repairers were making with the damaged boat, and had been told by them that it would be at least a week before it was seaworthy again. With a grim nod Daniel had proceeded to the hospital where Ely was and had been relieved to find him much better.

The old man's face lit up when he saw him and the first thing he said was, 'I know about the boat,

Daniel. Those young scallywags will get the length of my tongue when I get out of here. A couple of them came to visit me this morning and let the cat out of the bag because Bridget has been keeping quiet about it.'

'Did they tell you that two of their friends are in Oceans House with injuries from the accident?' Daniel questioned.

'Aye, they did,' he was told. 'They'll have to do better than that if they want to be in the lifeboat crew when they're older. Has it been called out at all while I've been in here?'

'No,' his visitor said, 'for which I'm thankful, as we both know the need for sea rescue can be sudden and dangerous to undertake, but at the moment all is calm.' Daniel got to his feet. 'I'm going to leave you now, Ely, and go for a bite at one of the places on the promenade to save me bothering when I get home. I'll call to see you again soon and in the meantime take care.'

'Aye,' he agreed, 'and you take care too. I'm expecting to be discharged in a week or so.'

As he drove along the promenade Daniel was half expecting to see Darcey Howard, as on other occasions, somewhere along the way, but not this time, and as he ordered a meal in his chosen restaurant the memory surfaced of how his second-in-command Brendan Stokes had been trying to chat her up when they'd arrived at the children's ward that morning and how her lack of response had made him hide a smile.

But he was far from relaxed about the new ward sister's seeming lack of family and friends. Was the romance she'd mentioned still off? Was that why she sometimes seemed remote? he wondered, and had to remind himself that it was absolutely nothing to do with him. He had his own life sorted and wasn't looking for any side turnings.

The grip of winter was taking hold as October made way for November and Darcey was not looking forward to Christmas. Alexander had been in touch briefly to say that they were having a great time so far with no mention of being home for Christmas or the New Year.

When he asked what plans she had made for the festive season she was vague, not wanting to tell him that she hadn't got any and that being so had volunteered along with others to work over Christmas and the New Year to give staff with families time with their loved ones.

She was surprised when one Friday morning in early November, Daniel took her to one side when he had finished his rounds and said with a smile, 'The boat is now seaworthy again. Some of the club members with me in charge are taking it for a sail down the coast some time over Christmas, and remembering your comment about your brother's interest in that sort of thing I wondered if you would like to come with us instead as he isn't around to join us.

'Some of the young ones seem to be at a loose end on Boxing Day so I thought maybe to go sailing then if the weather is suitable. That is if you're free, of course, as I'm aware that Christmas is a busy time for most people.'

Darcey could feel her colour rising. The last thing she wanted was to have to explain to him that she was so lonely that she'd volunteered to work all over Christmas. So instead she told him truthfully that she would be otherwise engaged elsewhere.

'Thank you for asking me,' she said weakly. 'It was a very kind thought, but I won't be free any time over Christmas. I'm fully booked, I'm afraid.'

She saw surprise in his expression and thought that she could at least have explained why she wouldn't be available, but there was no way she wanted anyone to know how alone she was, least of all him.

Daniel Osbourne had probably never had anyone of her sex not want to be with him, though it hadn't exactly been for a date, she reminded herself. The other two nurses she'd been with that night had described him as a loner. There would have been a boat full of teenagers to keep them apart if she'd accepted the offer.

'That's fine, then, if you aren't going to be alone,' he said levelly, and went on his way.

When he'd gone Darcey could have wept with

shame at the way she'd thrown his concern back in his face, but the fact remained that she just couldn't have admitted what a miserable thing her life was at the present time, and if Daniel Osbourne was the loner that she'd been told he was, maybe he was also going to be on his own during the festivities, which would make her refusal of his suggestion even more bizarre.

Though having seen his sister and her children briefly, and in spite of the haste with which she herself had made her exit, she had noted the affection between them that day when they'd called to see him, so it seemed hardly likely.

The day, like any other when she was on duty, was demanding her time, energy and patience, and she put the unexpected conversation they'd just had to the back of her mind until such time as when she would be free to absorb it fully, which was fortunate as at that moment a ten-year-old boy was admitted to the ward in pain and fractious with the osteomyelitis, which was more common in children than adults.

Daniel had seen Evan Roberts in his clinic and given orders for him to be admitted to the children's ward and given a course of antibiotics to clear the inflammation, and as Darcey and her staff followed his instructions and comforted Evan, there was an ache inside her at the memory of how she'd been so quick to refuse to sail in the ex-navy whaler that his club practised in.

Her reply to the effect that she was already going to be occupied on that occasion had been the truth and the reason for it had been understandable as far as she was concerned, having volunteered to work during the most important days of Christmas.

But would she have made that sort of commitment if she'd known that he was going to want to take her sailing, and what would he say should she tell him that she would love to go with him on some other occasion when she was free as long as the offer wasn't made out of pity because of her solitary state.

Daniel had referred to the lifeboat on a few occasions, a bigger and more powerful craft than his club used, as theirs was involved more in the safety of local events, and the thought of it made her keen to know more about the man who had come into her life on a crowded passenger train.

As she was leaving the ward after checking on Evan and having handed his care over to the night staff, Darcey saw Daniel glance unsmilingly in her direction as he went to speak to one of them, leaving her to make her way home with the feeling that it was going to be a miserable evening and if that was what it turned out to be, she had only herself to blame. With that thought in mind she decided to eat out at one of the restaurants on the promenade to delay enduring the gloom of the evening ahead any more than she had to and went to the nearest one, only to discover that it wasn't a good plan as just as she was about to enjoy the food put before her, Brendan Stokes appeared. Looking down at her upturned face, he said, 'Hi, Darcey. Do you mind if I join you?'

Before she could say yes, no or maybe, he was seated opposite and was beckoning to a nearby waitress who had eyes only for a customer who had just presented himself at a table at the other side of the restaurant but had paused to answer his phone, and as Darcey followed the woman's gaze she stifled a groan.

Why hadn't it occurred to her? she thought. It was to be expected that staff from Oceans House who had been working all day would choose the nearest restaurant, as had been the case on the night she'd dined with the two nurses.

'The boss just appeared,' her unwelcome companion said. 'He hasn't had much to say today, but it's clear that someone has rubbed him up the wrong way.' As she glanced over again, she saw Daniel abruptly standing and preparing to leave. 'Look, he's no sooner arrived than he's going, which I suspect will turn out to be a lifeboat alert.'

'So tell me about Mr Osbourne's connection with the lifeboat service,' she said. 'How does he come to be part of it?'

'His father was in charge at one time, him and old Ely were the main crew members, and when he died a couple of years back Daniel agreed to fill the gap his passing had left.

'He and Ely are hoping that some day new members of the lifeboat crew will come from their Young Sailors' Club, but their antics while he's been away haven't exactly filled him with confidence.'

As he turned to leave, Daniel glanced across and saw Darcey and Brendan dining cosily together, it seemed, and his jaw tightened. Was his second-in-command the reason for Darcey's fully booked Christmas, he thought grimly, the womaniser who never missed a trick if an attractive member of the opposite sex was anywhere near? Had the apparent lack of interest she'd shown when Brendan Stokes had eyed her up on his rounds merely been a pretence?

He had entered the restaurant by another door, but in leaving he passed their table and with a brief nod was gone in answer to the request for his presence on the lifeboat, taking with him the thought that she was the first woman he had even looked at since Katrina's welcome departure, and he might have been on the way to making another big mistake.

CHAPTER THREE

BACK IN THE restaurant Darcey was leaving the food on her plate untouched, and observing it her unwelcome fellow diner said, 'It's like I told you, the boss hasn't been his usual self today for some reason. Why don't we two make a night of it while he's riding the waves?'

She rose to her feet and said briefly, 'No, thanks. I'm going. It's been a long day and I'm tired.' And before he could comment further she had called the waitress over, paid the bill, and was on her way back to her accommodation.

On her way home Darcey heard someone say that the coastguards had been onto the lifeboat station to report that a yacht was in trouble out in the bay, and within minutes Daniel and the rest of the crew were kitted out and ready to sail into the winter night with all speed, while back in her small apartment Darcey crouched by the window that overlooked the sea and prayed that they would soon return with the boat and its occupants brought to safety, and after what seemed an eternity she saw white sails in the light of a pale moon with the lifeboat alongside, and sent up a prayer of thanks for all those concerned.

Especially for the man who had spent a busy day working in Oceans House, making good the problems of others, then had gone without the meal that he must have been more than ready for to take part in a situation that could have been dangerous in the extreme. As she closed the curtains and readied herself for bed she prayed that Brendan Stokes would not turn the incident of Daniel Osbourne's seeing them together in the restaurant into a tale of false innuendos.

The day's happenings had made her realise just how much Daniel's good opinion of her mattered to her and with that thought came the memory of her glib refusal of a sail with him and some of his club members during the festive season, giving him the impression that she would be living it up all over Christmas.

When he appeared the next morning she flashed him a tentative smile as he began his rounds but was met with a brief nod as he went from bed to bed, checking his young patients and passing on to her his requirements regarding them where necessary. Darcey felt that the only good thing to be happening was the absence of her dining companion of the night before, who, it appeared, was going to be away on a course for the coming week.

Daniel was determined to remain coolly professional towards Darcey. The sighting of her with

Brendan in the restaurant the night before had made him think how mistaken he'd been about her, after seeing her ignore Brendan on the ward only to find her dining with him happily enough at the end of their working day. No doubt that was the reason why she was fully booked for the activities of Christmas.

As for himself he had almost been on the point of changing his mind regarding his solitary existence, only to discover that she had an agenda of her own that he had known nothing about. The tired traveller on the train journey of not so long ago was turning out to be anything but short of company by the looks of it.

On the following Saturday Darcey was free from hospital duty and leaving the promenade behind went shopping in the town for food and other necessities, and once that was done she went into a nearby café for afternoon tea with the idea of delaying her return to the emptiness of her living quarters.

As she looked around her a woman seated at the next table smiled in her direction and as she acknowledged the gesture from a stranger with a smile of her own Darcey felt she looked vaguely familiar, and a flashback of herself zooming down the hospital corridor where Daniel Osbourne was chatting to his sister and her family, as she'd discovered afterwards, came to her.

'Would you mind if I join you?' the woman asked.

'No, not at all. I would be glad of the company,'

Darcey told her, and thought if this was who she thought she was maybe she might get to know something more about the man who was in her thoughts more than was good for her.

The woman introduced herself as Cordelia, and seated herself beside her. 'I remember seeing you at Oceans House's Orthopaedic Centre not long ago. My children and I had called briefly to see my brother, who is a great favourite with my little girls, and you went past us on the corridor, I recall.'

'Er…yes, that was me,' Darcey told her. 'I didn't want to intrude and quickly made my departure.'

'How long have you worked at the centre?' Cordelia questioned.

'Just a matter of weeks,' replied Darcey.

'And do you like it there?'

Darcey frowned slightly. 'Yes, and no. It can be quite lonely as I spend nearly all my free time on my own, which is only to be expected when one is living in a strange place, I suppose, but I love the job. When I saw a vacancy advertised for a ward sister at a coastal resort I didn't hesitate, and basically I have no regrets.'

'Would you like to dine with us one evening during Christmas to break the monotony?' Cordelia asked. 'I could invite Daniel along to swell the numbers.'

Darcey felt her face flush. 'It is very kind of you to invite me,' she said hastily, 'but I feel that Dr Osbourne wouldn't like it as he sees enough of me on the ward, without my intruding into his private life.'

'All right, if that is how you feel,' Cordelia said understandingly. 'But do let me know if you change your mind. Now I must go. My husband has taken our daughters out for the afternoon and they'll be back soon and ready for a meal. But one last thing before I go, what is your name?'

'Darcey Howard,' she said, with the feeling that she was getting out of her depth.

'Well, it has been nice to meet you,' the other woman said, and with that she was gone, leaving Darcey to visualise Daniel Osbourne's expression if he found himself thrown together with her socially after the chill he was bringing with him every time he entered the ward.

She went overboard with the shopping and as she stepped off one of the trams that ran along the promenade she pointed herself and her bags in the direction of her apartment, only to be brought to a halt momentarily as Daniel came walking towards her out of the hospital's main entrance. Observing her heavy load, he stopped to say, 'Let me take those for you, Darcey,' and as she hesitated, 'Have you started shopping for Christmas already?'

'Maybe just a couple of things,' she admitted as he took her shopping from her, 'but most of it was a weekly shop for the basics. Yet I did find time to have afternoon tea while I was out, which was nice, and while there I had the pleasure of getting to know your sister.'

She saw the dark hazel of his eyes widen, but his voice was calm enough as he said, 'You met Cordelia? How did that come about?'

'She was sitting at the next table and recognised me from the afternoon when she and your nieces called at Oceans House to see you, and the two of us had a nice long chat.'

'Not about me, I hope?' he questioned, and now his voice was cool.

'Well, maybe just a little, I suppose,' Darcey admitted uncomfortably. 'She invited me to dine with them and yourself some evening over Christmas but I felt that you might see enough of me during the day at the hospital without another appearance later.'

'That is as it may be, but aren't you all booked up over Christmas, if I remember rightly?' he said smoothly, and the moment to tell him the truth of what exactly she would be doing passed by because she was hurt to think that the man who was like no other she had ever met might be pairing her off with someone like Brendan Stokes.

'Yes, I suppose there is that. I can't let someone down at the last moment,' she agreed, with the thought in mind that it was only herself that she was letting down by not telling him the truth, that because she had no friends to turn to over Christmas she was going to give instead of take by being with the sick young ones in her care, and that an evening spent with him and his family would be something to hang onto in her loneliness.

But they were at the door of her apartment. Daniel was placing her shopping carefully on the step ready to be off and Darcey knew she couldn't beg for his company and that of his family, even if she never spoke to a soul over Christmas other than her young patients and their families.

As they faced each other she thanked him for carrying her shopping and, unaware of how much their unexpected meeting meant to her, he gave a brief farewell and was gone.

It was Ely's first night back with them after his illness and Daniel had been home to change his clothes before the evening ahead when he'd seen Darcey get off the tram and had found himself searching around for an excuse to linger and then thought better of it, but it didn't stop him from wondering what Cordelia was up to.

He knew that his sister wasn't happy about his solitary life but it was his choice, and even if he was attracted to Darcey Howard, so what? He hadn't forgotten seeing her and Brendan Stokes all cosy together in the restaurant, and he'd noted that Stokes had booked the time off way back to make sure that he wasn't caught up in the work zone during the festive season.

As Darcey unpacked her shopping the thought was there that Daniel hadn't been bursting to socialise with her at his sister's house during Christmas, which was not surprising, she supposed, if he was the loner that he appeared to be.

But what was it that he was expecting of her if she did? That she would pin him down beneath the mistletoe? Expect him to be dressed up as Santa Claus? Or that she might turn up looking like a Christmas fairy?

She'd done that several times when Alexander had been small and crying for his mother. But none of that was likely. If he was a touch-me-not, so was she, and on that thought she resigned herself to another lonely evening.

It had been great having Ely back amongst them at the club, Daniel thought as he made his way home after the meeting, and to make it even better the first of the two injured youths had been discharged by him from Oceans House and been well enough to attend, which left just one missing member, and Daniel was hoping that soon he too would be ready to leave the hospital, having also had time to dwell on their recklessness in taking the boat out without supervision.

It was cold, frost was glinting on the pavements and rooftops, and all the eating and drinking places on the promenade were full of those seeking warmth and company on a November night. Tempted by the scenes around him Daniel decided that a hot supper would be just the thing on such an occasion with the right company if possible and his thoughts went to Darcey who he had left earlier.

Would she be in or out? he wondered. And what would she think if he was to knock on her door to find out?

It had been as she'd expected, Darcey was thinking, a boring and lonely Saturday evening with no doubt many more to come, and as she gazed out of her window into the dark night her eyes widened as she observed Daniel walking purposefully towards her front door in the light of a nearby streetlamp, and when she opened it in answer to his knock he said, 'Can I come in? I thought you might have gone to bed but it seems not.'

'Is something wrong?' she asked in amazed enquiry.

He was smiling. 'Only if you say no.'

'What?' she exclaimed. 'I don't understand. Why have you come?'

'I was walking home from the club, in high spirits I may add because it has been a great night with Ely back amongst us, along with one of the lads that I've been able to discharge from Oceans House, and I suddenly felt the need of a hot supper but didn't fancy eating alone. Knowing that you live quite near to all the night life of the area I wondered if you would like to join me?'

'But I'm not dressed for the occasion,' she protested, 'and why me?'

'I've just explained that you were the nearest person to ask. So what do you say? All you have to do is put on a warm coat and off we go.'

'Yes, all right,' she agreed slowly. 'It has been a long, boring evening so maybe I'm ready for a change of scene, just as long as you're sure.'

Unexpectedly, Daniel felt his heart lifting. 'I'm sure,' he said. 'What do I have to do to convince you? The place we go to can be your choice.' He was tempted to comment, *As long as it isn't where I saw you with Brendan Stokes*, but thought better of it as that would put the dampener on the moment, if anything did.

'Where do you usually dine?' she asked as they left for the bright lights of the promenade. 'You know the place so much better than I do.'

'Right here,' he said, pausing outside the upmarket restaurant that was always his choice, unless it was at the end of an extra busy day at the hospital.

If that was the case he went to the first one he came to as he had done on the night when he'd seen her with Brendan.

'So do you want to try it?' he questioned.

'Oh, yes, please!' she said with eyes shining at the suggestion, and Daniel thought how different she was now from the weary traveller of that day on the train. Yet he still didn't know anything about her background. The only family member she'd mentioned had been her young brother, but surely there were others?

He was rather short on the ground with relatives himself, but Cordelia and her family were joy untold to have near so what more could he ask? And as the answer to that question surged forth, he pushed it to the back of his mind.

Of course he wanted children of his own, much as he loved his young nieces, but children needed a mother, which was a gap that he couldn't ever see himself filling, and with regard to his curiosity regarding Darcey's family, maybe that was where she was planning to go over Christmas, the thought of which would be much easier to contend with than days and maybe nights imagining her with Brendan Stokes.

Darcey observed Daniel, wondering what was going through his mind, as they studied the menu, and was on the point of finding out when he spoke.

'What are your family planning for over Christmas?' he asked casually, and she hoped she'd managed to hide the raw hurt that question caused.

'If you mean my brother, he's spending some time in Thailand over Christmas with a couple of friends. It's the first time we have ever been apart at this time of year and I'm missing him. The three of them have been bitten by the travel bug, which has left me alone, and if that sounds self-pitying I can't help it.'

'So what do your parents say about that?' he enquired.

'They are dead,' she told him flatly. 'I've brought Alex up since he was eight years old. There has just been the two of us and we've been happy enough, though I've known all along that one day he would want to branch out on his own, but didn't expect that it would be so soon.'

A waiter was approaching to take their order and when that had been accomplished she said, 'And that is it, but the trouble about caring is that it can come to be a habit that isn't easily broken.'

'Yes,' he agreed, 'and a burden that one can't easily be free of. I know because I've been there. But I haven't coaxed you out into the frosty night to depress you,' he said gently, 'and, Darcey, the young folk of today should be able to cope.'

'I know,' she agreed. 'I'm the one who isn't coping and I suppose I should know better.'

He reached across and stroking her hand said gently, 'There wouldn't have been many teenage girls prepared to do what you did for your young brother, to have been there for him until he reached manhood.

'So don't have any feelings of remorse. Instead be proud of yourself and watch as he becomes the man that your parents would have wanted him to be through you.'

As the food they had ordered, a veritable feast, was placed in front of them, and the man sitting opposite seemed more like a friend than a senior medical figure, or mentor of a group of young would-be sailors, Darcey couldn't believe how much she was enjoying the unexpected invitation to join him for a hot supper in a first-class restaurant. The only flaw was that he hadn't given her time to dress up for the occasion.

It would be something to remember in the long dark nights of winter when she was alone, and she hoped that the man sitting opposite hadn't invited her to dine with him because he felt sorry for her.

'So how do you like being based in Seahaven?' he asked as she gazed around her. 'Is the absence of your young brother taking the pleasure out of it in any way?'

Her smile was wry as she told him, 'Yes, I suppose I could say that because there has been just the two of us for so long I'm finding it hard to let go, but I'm finally seeing sense, as after all the only thing I want for him is that he should be happy, and that is what he is at present.'

'And what about you? Are you happy, Darcey?' he questioned gravely.

'At this moment I'm in heaven,' she told him recklessly, and when he had no comment to make lapsed into silence with the feeling that she had overdone the rapture somewhat on the strength of a nice meal in elegant surroundings.

As they walked towards her home when the meal was over and midnight was approaching, there was silence between them. The pleasure of the evening was disappearing fast as Darcey reminded herself uncomfortably that Daniel had only taken her for a meal to fill a gap.

That from what she'd heard, he was strictly off

liaisons with her sex, and when they reached her door she turned the key quickly in the lock and at the same time thanked him for the meal, then was gone before she made any more unwanted comments.

They were there again when Daniel opened his door some minutes later, the silent rooms, the lack of a woman's touch that he'd never had any problems with since Katrina's departure. But now he was wanting it gone, and of all things that he didn't want at that moment was for the phone to ring with a message for the lifeboat crew to tell them to be on the alert for a turn-out call to a stranded pleasure steamer that was having problems that it might be able to sort out, or it might not. When all he wanted was to sit quietly and remember the moments he'd just spent in the company of a woman who, it seemed, had got her priorities right.

How much had she given up, he wondered, in caring for her brother over the years? There were no rings on her fingers, wedding, engagement or otherwise, he'd been relieved to see. But was he getting carried away by her sense of duty to a parentless youngster, or was it the attraction of the sexes that he had avoided ever since the nightmare of Katrina that was out to snare him?

The phone rang again and there was good news. The pleasure steamer had arrived safely in the harbour and after some repairs would soon be on its way again. Relieved, he went slowly up the stairs to bed but not before he'd glanced to where not so far away there was still a light on in Darcey's apartment.

He wondered if she, like him, was going to put the evening down to a one-off, not to be repeated. There was still the memory of the hurt that a broken marriage brought with it as a warning and with that thought in mind he lifted the bedcovers and sought sleep.

In her own small abode Darcey was cringing at the thought of how she'd been so over-enthusiastic in her comments about the occasion that she'd found herself in, but it had been true. It had been heavenly to be wining and dining with a man for whom she had much respect for his work at Oceans House, and who was extremely attractive too, as that kind of situation had been almost non-existent before she'd changed her job for the delights of Seahaven.

Her position of ward sister in a local hospital had been just as demanding as the present one, and the rest of the time she'd spent trying to make up to Alexander for the loss of his parents, so that wining and dining with members of the opposite sex had been a rarity, hence her enthusiasm when she'd replied to Daniel's invitation.

But now she was wishing she hadn't been so forthcoming in her enjoyment of the occasion. It had made her sound naïve and had caused his lapse into silence that had continued until he had wished her goodnight on her doorstep and gone on his way.

The next time they met would be on the ward and she decided that when that happened she would show a restraint in her manner that couldn't possibly offend.

She was on duty tomorrow but Daniel Osbourne was only on call on Sundays for emergencies that only he could deal with, so it would be Monday before they met again and the job would come before anything else as they nursed and healed the young ones in their care.

On his way to his usual Sunday meeting at the boathouse, Daniel halted as Oceans House came into sight, and with sudden determination he pointed himself towards its main entrance, knowing that he was about to act totally out of character, but he had to see his dining companion of the previous evening, if only for a few moments in which to tell her that he had enjoyed her company.

His assurance might sound trite after he'd ignored her pleasure on the occasion but, sweet and vulnerable, she was hurting from the lack of her brother's company and he hadn't helped by withdrawing into his shell to combat her enthusiasm, which had brought him onto the defensive.

Darcey was with a trainee nurse when he arrived at the ward, showing her the facilities available for the care of the young with orthopaedic problems and as the two of them moved to the bed nearest to the door she saw him standing there and her eyes widened in surprised dismay.

She appeared to be waiting for him to speak first and, taking the hint, Daniel said, 'Just a word before I go to the Young Sailors' Club, Sister Howard,' and with a glance at the trainee nurse at her side, added, 'It will only take a moment.' Beckoning Darcey to follow, he went into the ward office and waited for her to come in.

When she'd closed the door behind her and was observing him warily he said, 'I've stopped by for a moment to thank you for your company last night. I requested it without giving you any warning and have since felt that I could have been more sociable, so I do apologise. I feel sure that you would have been much happier in the company of my colleague, who is due back amongst us in a week's time.'

Darcey wasn't ready to present her new personality of restraint in his presence. He was a day too soon, and the vows that she'd made the night before when he'd gone on his way after their silent walk home from the restaurant were not going to see the light of day, she thought, not after that comment. She told him, 'I am here to work, Mr Osbourne, not to find myself a man friend or lover, and if I were, the person you just mentioned would not be of my choosing. So now, if I may be excused, I am spending some time this morning with a trainee while the rest of the staff carry on as usual.'

Daniel stared at her, then nodded. 'Fine,' he said.

'Proceed, by all means.' As he watched her return to where she had been occupied he was aware of what he was missing in his determination never to be hurt again by a woman, and added to that Darcey Howard must think him an interfering bossyboots into the bargain.

But he had other matters to deal with in the next few hours that were separate from everything else in his life. They were different from any other thing he had ever done before and were in memory of his father, who had perished while saving the lives of others in a terrible storm.

He had lost his mother some time previously and he and his father had been very close, with both of them having a love of the sea, and he was getting used to the idea that the lighthouse just a mile up the coast and no longer in use, having served its purpose in bygone years, now belonged to him for whatever purpose he had in mind. It stood on a clifftop like a lonely guardian angel and there was the desire in him to bring it back to life in some way, which he hadn't yet decided upon, that would be a tribute to his father.

Up to the previous night he'd thought that a woman's perspective might be worth seeking with regard to his plans for the derelict building, but the opportunity hadn't materialised so far, and now that he and Darcey were at odds with each other, he felt it would be better to avoid the issue and stick to their doctor-nurse relationship. But it wasn't going to prevent him from being curious with regard to her fully booked-up Christmas if she wasn't chummy with Brendan Stokes after all.

CHAPTER FOUR

IT WAS OLD and neglected, Daniel thought as he surveyed the lighthouse keenly, but in a beautiful position. It had promise, and with some thought and expense could be transformed into a few things in its position high up on the cliffs.

He was going to rename it after his father Mark Osbourne, who had put the safety of others before his own, and he took detailed notes regarding the repairs needed as he walked slowly back along the top of the cliffs deep in thought, until he came to where the Sunday afternoon meeting of the Young Sailors' Club was in progress and put the challenge of the lighthouse out of his mind for the time being.

As the day progressed Darcey was finding it hard to forget their brief exchange of words in the ward office but she was not repentant. She'd had very few friendships with the opposite sex because of her responsibilities to Alexander and had never been bowled over by anyone she'd met.

But from the moment of their meeting on the train

she'd been so aware of Daniel Osbourne it was like a bright light in the midst of darkness, and that he should have coupled her with someone like Brendan Stokes had been mortifying, to say the least.

Maybe she'd been expecting too much in her new-found freedom from caring for Alex, she thought. Daniel was the top orthopaedic surgeon in the hospital, she was a ward sister, and they lived very different lives. But as the last few moments of a busy day presented themselves she thought rebelliously that she didn't need to have someone to take her to a nice restaurant if she wanted to dine there.

She decided she would go to the place where they'd dined the previous night on her own and if by any chance the man on her mind turned up, she would give him a Mona Lisa smile and continue to enjoy the food brought to her in all its excellence.

That thought died a death when a friendly waiter stopped by her table and commented, 'Your friend the doctor won't be joining you tonight, will he? We've been told that the lifeboat is out there and it's mighty rough.'

'And Daniel Osbourne is on it?' she questioned with her mouth dry and the food on her plate losing its appeal.

'Well, yes,' she was told. 'He's taken his father's place and in spite of all the demands of his work at Oceans House he never hesitates when he's asked to turn out with it. He is highly respected in these parts.'

'Yes, he must be,' she murmured, and asked for the bill with the urge to be some place where she could be alone while it registered how much she cared about him. Their skirmish earlier in the day was as nothing when she faced up to how much he was always in her thoughts.

She'd never been in love before and wasn't sure she really was in love now, or so she told herself as she went out into the cold night and pointed herself towards her small residence.

But once inside she couldn't settle and within moments was out again and was battling against strong winds towards the harbour, where relatives of the lifeboat crew and interested spectators were gathered with their gazes on the distant skyline for a glimpse of any sign of activity, but as yet there was none, and a group of Daniel's young trainees were huddled together in silent apprehension.

An elderly woman, with a calm that spoke of many such occasions, was passing round hot drinks that were being gratefully accepted by the watchers, and when she stopped beside Darcey she said, 'You have the look of somebody who has not seen this kind of thing before. Am I right?'

'Yes,' she said slowly. 'I'm a nurse from Oceans House and it is terrifying.

'What kind of situation has the lifeboat been called out to?'

'A couple of yachts with inexperienced crews have been caught unawares. If they manage to bring them back you might find some of them brought to the hospital if Daniel sees the need.'

At that moment a crew member who had stayed behind to keep in touch with the coastguard called, 'They've been spotted! Our crew have found them. One of the yachts has sunk and two of its crew were in the water when they got there, but they've hauled them aboard the lifeboat and are towing the one that's left. If they have no further problems they should be here soon.'

A couple of ambulances had arrived with their crews at the ready for possible casualties, and there were agonising moments that followed with Darcey not wanting Daniel to see her amongst those waiting for their return, but neither did she want to leave the scene until she had seen for herself that he was safely back on dry land.

So she waited until a cheer went up and as the rescue vessel came into sight, towing the remaining yacht behind it, with Daniel in full view she went, walking fast along the promenade where some of the restaurants and bars were still serving customers, unaware of the drama that had been unfolding at the end where the harbour was situated.

Darcey hadn't wanted to leave the scene there, yet neither had she wanted Daniel to see her amongst the crowd after their early morning exchange of words that had still been rankling. But as she went inside and locked the door behind her there was a great well of thankfulness inside her that was wiping out every thought except relief.

* * *

The ambulances had gone, taking both crews of the yachts to the town's main hospital to be checked over, and their arrival hadn't caused a great deal of surprise as the bay where Oceans House was situated was the source of a popular yachting competition every spring and those intending to enter were out in all weathers, practising before the event.

Back at the harbour there was the relief for the lifeboat crew of returning safely to hot soup, specially made by Bridget, to take away the chill of the last few hours, and on Daniel's part amazement to hear from her that one of the nurses from Oceans House had been there tense and concerned for their safety and his in particular.

'What was she like?' he asked. 'Did she say who she was?'

'Er...no, and I didn't think to ask,' Bridget told him. 'She was blonde with blue eyes that were filled with horror at the seriousness of what was happening, yet she went as soon as she knew that you were all safe.'

'I see,' he commented thoughtfully and asked himself if it was wishful thinking on his part that the first name that came to mind was that of Darcey Howard, though he had been so abrupt with her earlier that morning it was highly unlikely that she would have been concerning herself about him.

Unlike the night before, there was no pleasure to be had in knocking on her door. Neither was there any at the thought of returning to the peace of his apartment with its quiet comforts, as along with his verbal trespasses in her life he was tired.

It had been rough and dangerous out there in the bay, and on their return he'd been the only one of the crew who hadn't had an anxious relative waiting to welcome them back to safety, as he kept his lifeboat excursions as private as possible from Cordelia and her husband. Having lost the father she loved, he had no wish to cause his sister any further grief.

The only happy occasion that the day had brought had been his visit to the lighthouse that now belonged to him, and Daniel's last thought before he slept was that if she would let him, Darcey would be the first person to know about his recent purchase and it would be interesting to see her reaction.

On Monday morning Darcey gave Daniel a tentative smile that was tinged with the relief she was experiencing on seeing him his usual businesslike self when he was on the wards. She could cope with that where waiting for his return from the turbulent sea had been torture, especially so as she'd had no experience of that sort of thing before.

She'd gone before he had actually stepped on dry land because the last thing she'd wanted had been for him to think that she was making a nuisance of herself, and all the way back to her flat Darcey had been questioning silently how the families of the lifeboat crew coped on such occasions. The elderly lady stoically handing out refreshments to those who waited anxiously for their return had been very welcome.

There had been two fresh admissions to the children's ward that morning, a small boy with a fracture of his elbow and a teenage girl who had become unseated while horse riding, and as Daniel examined them Darcey felt that her world was righting itself after the traumas of the day before.

'Looking at the X Rays that have been taken, it is plain to see that young Harry's elbow is fractured so I'll get that sorted first as he has more damage to contend with than Ruby. Hopefully her neck will react to massage and heat to take away the pain. And, Sister, if we manage to get a lunch hour there is something I'd like to show you.' And off he went, leaving her to wonder what on earth he had meant by that.

She was more nervous in his company now than at any time since their meeting on the train that first day. She was so aware of him when he was near that she could hardly breathe and she had no idea what he could possibly want to show her.

It was a busy Monday morning for them both with regard to the children's ward, with Daniel setting Harry's elbow and then stabilising it in a cast, and afterwards instructing the nursing staff with Darcey in charge regarding the treatment for Ruby.

She had given up on finding time for a lunch hour, even though everything was in control on the ward, and was not expecting to see Daniel again, but he surprised her by appearing at the ward door and beckoning her across.

'Have you eaten?' he asked.

'Er…no, not yet,' she told him. 'I was just going to have a sandwich that I brought with me.'

'Would you be happy to eat it in the car?' was his next question.

'We need only be gone for a short time and after such a busy morning the staff will expect you to take a break.'

'Yes, all right,' she said, mystified, and went to get her coat.

They had driven past the harbour and the Young Sailors' Club and were now moving along the road at the top of the cliffs, with Darcey completely bewildered by what was happening, until Daniel stopped the car outside a disused lighthouse that incredibly had a sign outside that said 'Sold'. As she turned to face him in complete disbelief he said, 'You are looking at the new owner,' and glancing at his watch he added, 'There is just time for me to show you round before we return to Oceans House.'

As she walked slowly around the derelict building Darcey was speechless as she observed its condition, until finally, on the point of leaving, she gasped, 'Why?'

Daniel smiled. 'I can understand why you ask me that. A lot of other folk will be doing the same thing and the answer is that I'm going to have the whole place renovated in memory of my dad.'

'Ah, yes. I see,' she said gently. 'That I can understand. I think it's a lovely idea. If I can help in any way you have only to ask.'

'You were the one whose comments I wanted to hear,' he told her, 'as from what you've told me of your life so far it would seem that it has been one of giving rather than taking. And now I'm going to drive you back to where we belong.'

He wanted to ask if she had been amongst the crowd awaiting the return of the lifeboat the night before, but felt that today's gesture had been enough.

There was no way he wanted to give Darcey any wrong impressions.

But Darcey had a question to ask as they drove the short distance back to the hospital, and it was to be expected. 'Do your sister and her husband know about your plans for the lighthouse?' she asked.

'No,' he said firmly. 'I will tell Cordelia and Lawrence when it is done and ready for viewing. She wouldn't approve of its present condition one bit, but when she sees that it is named the Mark Osbourne Lighthouse she will be pleased, so I'd be obliged if you don't mention what I'm up to if you should happen to be in conversation with her again.'

The fact of their absence together during the lunch hour had been noted on the ward and there was a comment passed in Darcey's hearing to the effect that Daniel would be a hard nut to crack for anyone with hopes of becoming the second Mrs Osbourne, that he was content in the life he had chosen, and no one seemed to want to disagree with that.

As far as she was concerned, Darcey had no hopes whatever of someone like Daniel even noticing her, but it didn't stop her from rejoicing to have been asked for her opinion about his decision to buy the old lighthouse.

She could live with that and the fact that it was her that Daniel Osbourne had invited out to supper when he'd been on his way home from the sailing club, and if as a result she was falling in love with him she would just have to accept it and suffer in silence.

But that evening alone in the apartment, with not the slightest yearning to venture forth as she had been doing of late, Darcey began to think about Christmas. It was early December. All along the promenade were decorations celebrating the event and it was going to be the first time she hadn't spent the occasion with Alexander.

Instead she would be working during both Christmas Day and Boxing Day, and solitary in the evening, and if Daniel Osbourne came across her in such circumstances what was he going to think about her refusal to go sailing with him and his club members?

Yet the fact remained that when he'd extended the invitation she had already committed herself to working during the festivities, and somebody had to do it so why not her with no family ties or suchlike to prevent her? And she would make sure that her small patients who had to spend Christmas in Oceans House had as happy a time as possible under the circumstances.

She knew she had to keep her feelings for Daniel Osbourne strictly under control to avoid making a fool of herself, as every time she thought about their lunchtime trip to the lighthouse she felt tearful because he was so special and so out of reach.

In the meantime, she needed to shop for a special Christmas gift for Alexander to be presented whenever he chose to return. It was her day off and the shopping didn't take long, with only two to buy for, and as Darcey waited to be served at the till in one of the stores in the town centre, Cordelia Mason appeared laden with parcels and wanting to know if she felt like joining her for a coffee.

She didn't hesitate to say yes because she liked Daniel's sister and felt that being in her company was the next best thing to his.

'We haven't seen much of Daniel for a while,' Cordelia said after they'd chatted about various small matters, 'which usually means that he is very busy at Oceans House, or with other things that he knows would upset me if I knew, such as taking Dad's place in the lifeboat, which he insists on doing, and pointing out that he has no wife or children of his own to concern himself over and that my two are safe and happy with Lawrence and me. So it wouldn't hurt anyone but himself if one time he didn't come back to dry land and safety, ignoring the fact that he would have made a fantastic husband and father if he hadn't married Katrina.'

As she listened to what Cordelia had to say, Darcey thought that he was wrong. There was someone else who would die a death if anything happened to Daniel even after so short an acquaintance, but she was in no position to make any comments to his sister, especially after his lovely gesture with regard to their father and the lighthouse.

'He is very busy most of the time at the hospital,' she said, without admitting that she had actually been present on a recent occasion, 'but he does sometimes get called out to help man the lifeboat, so I'm told.'

'Can I ask you to let me know if he is ever in any grave danger that I may not be aware of?' Cordelia asked anxiously, and with a reluctant nod Darcey prayed that such a day would never dawn.

His sister was checking the time and commented, 'I'm going to have to leave you, I'm afraid, Darcey. I'm due to pick the children up from school, but before I go just one thing, the invitation to visit us still stands whenever you can manage it. I hate to think of you all alone over Christmas. If you do find that you can spend some time with us, Daniel will give you our phone number and will drive you to where we live whenever the occasion arises.'

Darcey swallowed hard. There was no way she could get involved with those kind of arrangements.

There was the minor matter of her opting to work every day over the Christmas period, and he would take a dim view of the fabrication of the truth that she'd resorted to when he'd invited her to sail with him and some of the young sailors on Boxing Day, and then discovered what her plans were with regard to that.

On the strength of it the last thing he would opt for would be taking her to share her lonely evenings with his family and himself. She would rather exist without seeing a soul than gatecrash Daniel's time with those he loved, having checked the work rotas for the period and seen that he was only available for extreme emergencies. The day-to-day running of the hospital would be in the hands of two junior doctors and an elderly retired consultant who was volunteering his services to give Daniel a break.

When the two of them met up the next morning for their usual ward round Daniel said amicably, 'I believe you saw Cordelia again yesterday. It seems that she is still keen for you to visit some time during Christmas in spite of you being sorted. But I must warn you that she will have her matchmaking hat on as she longs for me to give up my bachelor status.'

Darcey felt the colour rise in her cheeks but her voice was cool as she told him, 'Thanks for the warning, but as I mentioned previously I will be booked up for most of the Christmas period.'

'With whom, might I ask?' he enquired abruptly,

and her eyes widened at his sudden interest in her affairs.

She looked around her at the collection of cots and beds and their young occupants and told him, 'I'll be with those I care for. What more could I ask?' And when their gazes held, his was wanting to know more than that, and hers was holding back the tears of her loneliness.

His rounds of the ward had been done without any further stresses and Daniel had gone to his own part of the hospital where he had his office and held his twice-weekly clinic, while Darcey and her staff went about their duties as usual.

But beneath her normal competence the ward sister was miserable and unhappy to have been warned off accepting Cordelia's invitation to dine with them because his sister was anxious to see him as married and happy as she was with her husband and children.

It was as if Daniel had warned her to keep her distance and it hurt as there was no way that she was going to seek his attention under the guise of visiting his family. She had more pride than that, was aware that if she hadn't devoted her life to her young brother she might have found love long ago. But she had no regrets about that. Alexander's needs had always come first.

Back in his own quarters at Oceans House Daniel was cringing at the way he'd made himself sound such a catch instead of a loner in the matrimonial stakes.

Since meeting Darcey Howard he'd been unsettled. His solitude was lying heavily upon him instead of being a comfort, and he'd just made sure that she wasn't going to want to be in his company outside hospital hours. Better to mention that to Cordelia and tell her to lay off the matchmaking as it could only make matters worse.

At the end of the day he stopped off at his sister's on his way home and found her in the kitchen, preparing the evening meal, and was immediately invited to share it with them.

'No, thanks just the same,' he told her gently. He cared for her too much to quarrel, but nevertheless wanted to make it clear that if ever he decided to involve himself in marrying again he would make all the moves and the proposals without any assistance from anyone else, and introduced the subject with the comment that Darcey had told him that they'd met up again and that Cordelia had repeated the invitation to join them some time over Christmas.

'Yes, I have,' she replied, 'because she is so lonely, Daniel.'

'That is not so,' he told her firmly. 'When I asked Darcey if she would like to sail with me and some of the kids on Boxing Day she was quick to explain that she was fully booked up all over the Christmas period. How, I don't know and wasn't prepared to ask. Maybe she could be planning to share it with her young brother if he will be back from abroad in time, but I really don't know. What I do know is that she has got Christmas sorted and is not the lost soul that you see her as.'

'All right,' she agreed. 'Maybe my imagination has been running riot, but if Darcey does decide to accept the offer, promise me that you will make her welcome.'

'Yes, of course!' he said, feeling rather affronted. 'What would you expect? That I would ignore her presence? Insist that she stand in a corner without speaking?'

He was hardly likely to inform Cordelia that Darcey Howard had captured his imagination ever since that day in the discomfort of a crowded railway carriage, and as he'd got to know her better the more she was in his thoughts, yet not to the extent that he was ready to give up his freedom from matrimony.

Young voices could be heard coming from up above, and putting the discussion they'd just had on hold Cordelia said laughingly, 'Your fan club have been watching television and will be down shortly. Are you sure that you don't want to stay?'

'Not this time,' he said. 'I have some business to attend to.' And to make up for leaving before the children appeared, he offered, 'How about I have them for the day on Saturday so that you and Lawrence can have some time for just the two of you during the day?'

'That would be lovely!' she exclaimed. 'But are you sure? You are always so busy.'

'Yes, I am sure,' he told her smilingly. 'I'll take them for a short sail in the club boat on Saturday morning and to a children's matinée at the cinema in the afternoon, as there is no meeting of the Young Sailors' Club this week. Its members have arranged a dinner dance in the evening at a large hotel on the promenade instead to help raise funds to pay for the repairs to the boat.' With an upward glance to where the children were playing, he gave his sister a quick kiss on her cheek. 'And now I must go.'

Daniel wasn't sure how good a case he had made with his sister regarding his private and public life-styles, and as he pulled up outside the place that he used to call home minutes later, he couldn't resist casting a glance in the direction of the hospital apartments to check if Darcey's light was on. Seeing its bright light glowing in the early evening darkness, he went inside feeling content.

CHAPTER FIVE

DANIEL WASN'T TO know that in the late afternoon after he had left the hospital to call at Cordelia's on the way home, some members of the sailing club had gone to Oceans House selling tickets for the event of the coming Saturday and that Darcey had bought one to brighten up her quiet life away from the hospital, with her first thought after making the purchase being what she was going to wear.

There was nothing suitable amongst the clothes she'd brought with her and the event was only days away, so she needed to move fast in the form of some late-night shopping. After a quick snack, she caught the promenade tram and went into the town centre in a frame of mind that was willing to be appealed to by what she saw, and appealed to it she was by a dress of turquoise silk that accentuated her golden fairness and the soft curves of her body. With shoes to match and a faux fur jacket to hold off the winter chill she was very pleased with her purchases.

* * *

Daniel had seen that Darcey's place was in darkness and, imagining her on the promenade on her own somewhere in the winter night, was unusually fraught and irritated at the thought, so instead of relaxing in the warm comfort of his apartment he drove along there a couple of times. After no sightings of her, he checked the nearest restaurants to make sure that she wasn't anywhere to be found.

Then, deciding that if he lingered any longer he might be accused of loitering, he was on the point of departing when he saw her moving fast towards her apartment building with a carrier bag from one of the boutiques swinging from her wrist. The question of where was she going to wear what she'd bought came immediately to mind with a vision of her somewhere in another man's arms.

Usually he didn't give a damn who he saw in those sorts of circumstances but every time he was near her the attraction of who and what she was brought back desires long dead, so he pointed his car homewards without letting her see him hovering nearby. As he drove the short distance the thought uppermost in his mind was, Who and what was she going to be occupied with all over Christmas?

When he arrived back at the apartment there was a message from the architect who was in charge of the renovation of the lighthouse, wanting to discuss various matters, and by the time Daniel had returned his call there was, as expected, a light where there had been darkness in her apartment, and for what was left of the evening he refrained from glancing in that direction.

The dinner dance was to be held at a large hotel in the town centre and tickets had been selling fast as the townsfolk were always ready to support any event connected with safety on the sea that surrounded Seahaven.

It was an event that Daniel was keeping a low profile on, which was perhaps as well because he was late arriving due to an accident victim with a spinal injury being brought into the hospital as he had been on the point of leaving, and he had stayed to perform the necessary surgery, followed by going home to change into evening wear.

Darcey, stunning in the new clothes she'd bought, and unaware of the reason for his non-appearance, was trying to keep Brendan Stokes, who had returned from his refresher course, at a distance with the thought in mind that without Daniel the event would mean nothing.

He came at last and she felt that her bones would melt with longing, but when he saw her he smiled briefly and went to talk to the elderly woman who had been handing out hot drinks on the night of the lifeboat rescue, and an elderly man she presumed was the lady's husband. On seeing her expression, her unwelcome companion commented, 'If the boss ever decides to tie the knot again, I wouldn't count on it being someone at the hospital.' And sauntered across the room to where a group of young women doctors was gathered.

Darcey watched him go and wished herself far away from the cheerful gathering of locals. She was a stranger in their midst, lost and lonely, and was contemplating a speedy departure when Daniel appeared beside her and said, 'Don't let Brendan Stokes upset you, Darcey, he's not worth it. As all the tables are full I came to ask if you would like to share with Bridget, Ely and myself?'

'I'd love to,' she said, smiling her pleasure, even though Bridget might remember her from the night when she'd been one of those frantically hoping for the safe return of the lifeboat and those it had gone to rescue.

When Daniel took her to be introduced to his friends Bridget did indeed remember her from the night when Darcey had stood white faced on the edge of the crowd, waiting anxiously for the return of the lifeboat. And now, seeing her with the man that she herself had much respect for, Bridget made no comment regarding that, just shook her hand and welcomed her warmly, while Ely looked on in disbelief at the sight of his friend with someone of the opposite sex. When Daniel took her onto the dance floor his surprise peaked, though not as much as Darcey's.

Darcey was so conscious of his touch and so aware of the surprised glances that were fixed on them as they moved around the floor that she was speechless, and he said with dry amusement, 'I just thought I'd give them something to talk about, the ones who would like to see me with a woman just out of curiosity.'

Daniel felt her stiffen in his arms and knew he'd hit a nerve, but he wanted some response from her, be it good or bad, and he was getting it as she broke away from his hold and went to join a group of nurses from Oceans House who were sitting at tables near the bar.

'What did you do to the lass?' Ely asked in amazement when Daniel rejoined his friends.

Bridget commented, 'Darcey was the nurse that I told you about who came to join those of us that night when the lifeboat had been called out. I recognised her when you brought her to meet us tonight. Do you remember me telling you?'

'Yes, vaguely,' Daniel replied, 'though I've got to know Darcey because she's the sister on the children's ward. But there's nothing going on between us. I brought her across to our table because she was on her own, that's all.'

'That's a disappointment, then,' Bridget told him. 'I'm always ready for a new outfit should I hear wedding bells.'

Daniel was only half listening. Darcey looked lovely beyond belief in the turquoise dress. Was that what was lacking in the empty life he had chosen with the break-up of his marriage? Someone like the caring nurse who had appeared out of nowhere on a crowded train?

He had wanted to hold Darcey close and would have continued to do so if he hadn't been irritated by the stares and smirks coming in their direction. Now the opportunity had gone and he had only himself to blame.

Looking across to where she'd been sitting, he saw that the place was empty and when he went into the hotel foyer he saw her in a taxi that was in the act of pulling away from the pavement outside, and as it drove off he flagged down the next one to arrive and told the driver to follow the vehicle in front.

Darcey was in the process of paying the taxi driver when the second vehicle pulled up behind it, and to her surprise she watched Daniel climb out. He said to her driver, 'I'll settle that,' and to his own driver, 'And yours too in a moment.' She observed him with a stony-faced expression as he dealt with the two fares. Once the vehicles had departed, he turned to find her putting her key in the lock with the intention of leaving him on the step.

'May I come inside for a moment?' he asked, and without speaking she stepped to one side to let him pass and then closed the door behind him.

'I just want to say I'm sorry if you felt I was using you to suit my own ends when I took you onto the dance floor,' he said as they faced each other in the apartment's small entrance hall.

'The reason was because you looked so beautiful in the dress and as we are both free spirits it felt like the right thing to do. But for some reason the fact of my having no desire to make a commitment in the marriage market is of interest to some people and irritates me more than somewhat. Someone once told me that when I do appear with a member of the opposite sex they place bets on whether it will last or not. So will you accept my apology for what happened back there, Darcey?'

'You don't have to apologise, Dr Osbourne,' she said stiffly. 'I have no wish to be involved in your private life and neither do I want to be made a laughing stock by those who are so interested in it.'

He groaned softly and reaching for the door handle ready to depart said, 'I can hardly blame you for feeling like that. My sister has yearnings to see me at the altar every time a possible candidate appears, but she knows how small the chances are of that happening, and if she hadn't, I would have soon put her right.'

Darcey thought if that was the case, what was it that she had done to deserve so much attention?

To make it even more upsetting, he went on to say, 'It would seem that you have already got Christmas lined up with friends past and present on the occasion of your first time of celebrating it by the sea, and if that is so I wish you a happy time amongst them.'

With a wild desire to tell him the truth about what she would be occupied with she moved towards him, but the door was swinging open, he was gone and no way was she going to chase after him, which left the next morning on the wards looming ahead like a pit of embarrassment.

Having no wish to make any further upsets for anyone, Daniel went straight home and sat gazing towards the light in Darcey's window. She was a sweet, kind woman, he told himself, and deserved better than such as himself, so the less he saw of her away from Oceans House the bigger the favour he would be doing her. Unaware that not so far away she was gazing across at the light in his window with a yearning to be with him, in his house, in his arms, in his life.

Darcey was spared the dread of meeting up with him again on Monday morning because Brendan Stokes was doing the ward rounds, Daniel having been called out to join the lifeboat crew on another mission to rescue some teenagers who were way out past the coastguard station, and when she discovered where he was and what he was engaged in, the stress of meeting him on the wards was as nothing compared to knowing that he was out in dangerous waters, fighting the elements again, and she loved him for it, just as she loved him for everything he did.

This time she couldn't be present when the lifeboat came back to base and was frantic to know if and when all concerned were safe, until Bridget stopped by the ward in the lunch hour to report that another stressful situation had been resolved. Grateful for the elderly woman's thoughtfulness, Darcey thought that she wasn't the only one who loved Daniel. So did Cordelia, and so did Bridget in a motherly sort of way, and with that thought came another.

She had made a reluctant promise to his sister that she would tell her if Daniel was involved in anything dangerous or stressful with regard to the lifeboat and today was the second occasion when she had failed to do so, not wanting to distress Cordelia.

With a few moments of her lunch break left, she went into the office on the ward and rang the number that his sister had given her, but got no answer and tried a few more times without success. Finally she gave the operator the number and asked to have it checked in case there was a problem on the line as now she was more than ready to talk to Cordelia as it would be only good news that she had to greet her with.

But the operator reported that the line was being investigated and it could take some time, and as Darcey replaced the receiver, Daniel was there framed in the open doorway, observing her unsmilingly and asking, 'What's wrong? Everyone is back safely. No cause for alarm, and that was Cordelia's number. Why? What goes on?'

'Er...your sister asked me to get in touch if ever you were hurt or in danger,' she said haltingly, 'but there has been no need, and in any case I would have hesitated to do anything of that nature, which was against your wishes, but I saw no harm in letting her know that you are safe after today's occurrence if she is aware of it.'

'I see,' he said tonelessly, and went on to inform her, 'The last thing I want would be to cause Cordelia grief on my account. She has already had to face up to us losing our father. I don't want any other sorrow coming her way because of me.'

'So why do you do it if that is how you feel?' she questioned.

'Because it is what he would have wanted of me.'

'Yes, I see,' she told him, and thought that Daniel was already doing his share of saving lives at Oceans House and many of them were young ones, which would be enough for most people, but he wasn't most people.

Around her the staff on second lunch were disappearing and as he hadn't eaten since breakfast he followed them and left her to thoughts that were not happy ones.

After lunch Daniel went to take his Monday afternoon clinic with the feeling that he had been needlessly abrupt in his conversation with Darcey, especially after the fiasco of the night before, and the thought came that flowers, roses maybe, with a note of apology attached, might clear the air between them without creating any more situations that she might have misunderstood.

As soon as the clinic was over he rang a florist and arranged for flowers to be delivered the next day, as the following morning he was due to fly out to America for two weeks, where he would be speaking to medical staff in various hospitals about orthopaedics, with the intention of arriving home on the day of Christmas Eve, when he had arranged to go straight to his sister's for the festivities, while Darcey was enjoying her first Christmas in Seahaven in what had sounded like a full programme of events when he'd suggested taking her for a sail and had had the offer turned down.

It was six o'clock the next morning and as the taxi that was taking him to the airport was driven along the deserted promenade for his flight to America Daniel was wishing that he wasn't going to be without sight of Darcey for two whole weeks.

There had been no signs of life as he'd been driven past her apartment, which wasn't surprising considering the hour, and his reluctance to be away from where she was going to be increased. In an hour or so the florist would do as he'd asked and deliver the flowers before she began her day's work, and what she would think of that he wasn't going to find out as she would have no way of knowing that they were the first flowers he'd sent to anyone of the opposite sex since his marriage to Katrina had fizzled out in a cloud of misery.

At the time of arranging the visit to various American hospitals he had been keen and raring to go, but now the thought of being away from Oceans House meant being away from her, and when he returned on Christmas Eve she was sure to be well into the Christmas festivities that she had planned, which could mean only one thing, that away from the job and in so short a time she had created a good social life, which was more than he could say for himself.

When there was a knock on the door of her apartment just before eight o'clock, Darcey paused in her preparations before heading for the children's ward for the day, and was presented with an assorted display of beautiful roses and lily of the valley with a card attached that said briefly, 'Sorry I was so unfriendly yesterday, Daniel.' Her heartbeat quickened at the comforting thought that in the middle of his last-minute arrangements for his departure he had taken the time to want peace between them, and her step had a lift to it as she walked the short distance to where she would be spending the day with her young patients.

On the Saturday in the middle of the fortnight of his absence, when she'd done her shopping Darcey went into the café where she'd first met his sister in the hope that they might meet again, and was happy to find Cordelia seated at one of the tables and beckoning her across to join her.

Desperate for news of Daniel, she was quick to

accept the invitation and heard how he was enjoying his visit to one of America's largest cities and being entertained socially every evening by those he was working with in the daytime.

The name of Mallory, a medical colleague over there, cropped up a few times and Darcey's pleasure in receiving the flowers that he'd sent on that last day shrivelled into nothingness.

But Cordelia had not forgotten her liking for the young nurse seated opposite and asked anxiously, 'Are you sure that you have a good time planned for Christmas, Darcey? You are most welcome to share it with us if you are short of company.'

'Yes. I've got it sorted,' she replied with false confidence, 'but thanks for the thought. You are very kind, Cordelia, and all my good wishes to you and your family.' On the way home afterwards she looked down at the shopping she was carrying and thought how it was just the usual weekly things with a box of chocolates as her only sign of festive fun, but that thought was followed by a vision of anxious parents beside the beds of their precious little ones at Christmas. Rather than feeling sorry for herself, she knew that to be there for them would be a privilege.

It was Christmas Eve a week later and Daniel was homeward bound in a taxi that would shortly be arriving at Seahaven, and much as he had enjoyed his visit to America he was eager to be back in the place he loved the most.

What would Darcey have planned for the evening? he wondered, as the promenade came into view with Oceans House at the far end. Whatever it was, it would not include him, from the sound of it, and as far as he was concerned if he hadn't been staying with Cordelia and her family over the festive break he would have gone straight home and to bed after the long flight.

But to the two small girls who loved him, his presence on Christmas morning added greatly to the excitement, so that he would never disappoint them willingly. And as for the nurse who had been in his thoughts more than was good for him while he'd been away, he supposed he should be happy for her to have settled into Seahaven so well that her Christmas was fully booked.

It would prevent him from stepping into something that he might regret afterwards, and with that thought came the memory of Darcey's eager response when he'd asked her if she was enjoying being taken unexpectedly to dine in his favourite restaurant that night.

It could have been the beginning of something special and precious if he'd responded with similar enthusiasm, but the barriers had been up, the warning signs had been there. He'd sat there poker faced as Darcey had made no secret of the pleasure that his unexpected invitation had created in her lonely life, and now he was wishing that he'd responded.

An attractive medical administrator called Mallory had accompanied him on his visits as he'd moved from one hospital to another. They'd also dined together in the evenings, and it had become clear that she'd been romantically interested in him.

But Daniel had thought grimly that, as pleasant a person as Mallory was, she was coming onto the wrong sort of guy as far as he was concerned, and in her place would come a vision of Darcey soothing a fretful toddler in the children's ward at Oceans House, and on another occasion gazing wide-eyed at the old lighthouse he'd bought in memory of his father with complete understanding of his need.

As the hospital came into view at that moment, with her small living quarters close by, he was tempted to pay the taxi driver and call on her if she was there, but the opportunity didn't arise. The place was in darkness. It seemed as if her busy Christmas was already under way.

In the two weeks that Daniel had been away, the friendship between Darcey and Cordelia had strengthened and they'd met for coffee a couple more times, with Cordelia inviting Darcey to the party that she and her husband were hosting on Christmas Eve.

But as Darcey had remembered the glib pronouncement that she'd come up with when Daniel had offered to take her sailing, and imagining his expression if he arrived back and saw her at the party, she had said, 'It is kind of you to invite me, Cordelia, but I really don't want to cause any difficult situations that could be avoided.'

'The party will finish at midnight,' her new friend hastened to tell her, 'and Daniel won't be back until the early hours of Christmas Day. I know you are concerned that he might think you are invading his privacy, but it should be long over before he puts in an appearance, so do come, Darcey. One of our daughters is keen to become a nurse when she is older, and will be asking you all sorts of questions about it before she goes to bed.'

'Yes, all right,' she'd agreed, unable to resist being with company on Christmas Eve, even if she was going to be alone for the rest of the holiday period, and if she would be well gone by the time Daniel put in an appearance there couldn't be any harm in having a happy evening for once, instead of another empty one.

There was just one snag to that arrangement, though. The last two weeks had been filled with the longing to have Daniel back where she could see him, but she wouldn't see him on Christmas Eve, according to Cordelia, and as he wasn't on the staff roster for over the holiday it could be some time before they came face to face again, unless she sought Daniel out with some excuse.

Darcey went to the party in the turquoise dress that had bowled him over on the evening of the effort to raise money for repairs to the rescue boat, and was feeling good to be socialising with a group of friendly folks at Lawrence and Cordelia's house.

But, like Cinderella, come midnight she had to leave, and with just a few moments to spare Darcey went round saying her farewells to her hosts and their friends, and then she was gone, striding purposefully along the brightly lit promenade to where her small dwelling awaited her, having refused the offers of a lift home from some of the party guests who would have liked to get to know her better.

As the taxi driver drove along the coast road on the way to Seahaven, the old lighthouse was silhouetted against a pale moon and Daniel felt a rush of tenderness at the memory of how Darcey had understood immediately how much it would mean to him to have a memory of the father so near and so dear to him.

The two weeks he'd been away had seemed like two years and once he was home there was no guarantee that she would be where he could see her if she had the Christmas break all planned, as it had seemed to be from what she'd said.

Ahead the promenade had come into sight and as the taxi moved nearer to his destination Daniel was observing groups of revellers out there, celebrating the midnight hour and the arrival of Christmas Day.

He had caught an earlier flight than previously arranged and within minutes would be back amongst his family and friends, but the one person he wanted to see the most would be doing her own thing somewhere else, and he would so like to know where.

No sooner had the thought crossed his mind than his wish was granted.

Darcey, wearing the lovely turquoise dress that he'd seen before and been enchanted by, under her coat, was walking briskly along the opposite side of the promenade, and he asked the taxi driver to stop for a moment. Flinging himself out of the vehicle with all speed, he followed her quickly on foot.

When she heard his footsteps behind her, she turned and stared at him in amazed dismay as he said with cool calm, 'What are you doing out here alone at this hour? Where are all the friends you're spending Christmas with?'

Seeming to recover from the shock of his sudden appearance, she told him, 'It's tomorrow that my busy time starts.'

'So where have you been?' Daniel asked with quiet impatience, wishing their reunion after an empty fortnight could be more ecstatic.

He could see the desperation in her eyes as she told him, 'I've been to a party at your sister's house on the promise that you wouldn't be back for a couple of hours, as I knew that you wouldn't want to find me there when you returned.'

'So you read my mind, do you?'

'Yes, up to a point,' she told him defiantly.

'I doubt it,' he said with silky slowness. 'Otherwise you would know what is coming next.' And as she gazed at him wide-eyed he pulled her into his arms and kissed her until she was limp and trembling, and only then did he let her go.

'Merry Christmas, Darcey', he said in a low voice, and beckoned the taxi driver to bring his vehicle to their side of the road. 'Get in,' he ordered, and as she obeyed, he told her, 'I'm going to see you safely home, and then will depart just in case you have any worries on that score.'

Daniel had asked the taxi driver to wait to take him the way he had come to his sister and brother-in-law's house a short distance away because his baggage was on board, but first he wanted to see Darcey safely inside. As she turned the door key of the apartment in the lock he said tonelessly, 'Have a good Christmas, Darcey. You're young and beautiful so should have no trouble with that.' Before she could reply he turned and hurried off into the night.

Sitting in the waiting taxi, he groaned softly and the driver asked conversationally, 'Was that your girlfriend, sir?'

'Er...no,' he told him. 'She is just a friend that I was expressing my good wishes for Christmas to,' and as the other man nodded understandingly Daniel lapsed into silence with the thought uppermost that he had just made a prize fool of himself.

Darcey was weeping, hunched beside the small gas fire in what served as her sitting room. Worries, he'd said! As if she would have any worries about Daniel's intentions, she thought tearfully. Longings, hope, yes, but not worries. It was a situation where Daniel was way out of her league and for the first time in her life she was in love, hopelessly, totally in love with a man whose failed marriage had left a bitter taste behind, so much so that a stray kiss of the kind they had shared would be the limit of his trust.

The moment she had longed for had just taken place. Daniel had kissed her long and meaningfully but without a word of love, and it had turned what might have been a moment of joy into something hurtful.

Or was she making a big thing out of something small? she asked herself bleakly, because her experience of such things was limited due to the burden of care she had carried for so long with regard to her young parentless brother?

Whatever the reason, she was relieved that after what had happened she would be tucked away at Oceans House during the days of Christmas, and in the evenings would find a way to pass the time somehow or other, even if it meant eating out on her own, and with that cheerful thought in mind she went to bed and was drifting into a restless sleep when the phone rang. When she picked it up, Alex's voice came over the line.

'Darcey! I've been trying to get through to wish you a merry Christmas for ages,' he said. 'Where have you been?'

'I've been to a party,' she told him, 'and haven't

been back long. I rang you a couple of times and had the same problem. Everyone is so busy at this time of year, I'm afraid. Where are you ringing from?'

'We're still in Thailand and I'm just returning to the hotel after having a great time. It's early morning here,' he informed her. 'We will be moving on after Christmas as we want to see as much of this country as possible before we come home, and the money won't last for ever. We'll probably be back by Easter.'

She was smiling, her loneliness forgotten for the moment as she told him, 'I'm so glad that you've been in touch and are well and happy. I've volunteered to work during Christmas to give staff who have young families some time with them, so if you need me for anything you will know where to find me. Now I have to say goodnight as I have to be on the ward at eight o'clock in the morning with all of Christmas Day to follow, so take care and have a good time with your friends.'

'I love you, big sister, and I'm sorry I was such a pain before you left,' he said in parting, and when Darcey lay back against the pillows again, the frustrations of earlier in the night didn't seem so hurtful. Maybe she'd been wanting too much from Daniel. Been longing too much to see him back in her life, and he'd had no such yearnings, so that the kiss out there on the promenade had just been a 'nice to see you' sort of gesture, and on that thought sleep came at last.

* * *

When Daniel arrived at his sister's house Cordelia and Lawrence were busy clearing up after the party, ready to bring down the children's Christmas presents from wherever they were hidden, and she exclaimed, 'Daniel! Did you get an earlier flight?'

'Yes,' he told her wryly, 'and who do you think I met on the promenade moving at a similar speed to Cinderella when she left the ball that time?'

'I have no idea,' she replied.

'Oh, yes, you have,' he protested gently, and as Lawrence turned away to hide a smile, 'You matchmaker! Didn't I tell you that Darcey had her Christmas fully arranged as from tomorrow? She will have been working today and then will be off for the rest of the festivities.'

'I invited her to the party because I thought you wouldn't be there,' Cordelia protested, 'not because I thought you would. And it was only when I told Darcey that you weren't due home until quite a while after twelve o'clock that she accepted the invitation to join us. What did she have to say when you met up like that?'

'Not a lot, just the usual pleasantries,' he told her casually. It was hardly the moment to explain that Darcey's lack of conversation had been due to the fact that she'd been unable to get a word in edgeways as he'd been kissing her most of the time. For what had seemed like a delightful eternity he'd held a lovely woman close and had got it all wrong. Was he so out of practice?

Climbing the stairs to the immaculate bedroom that was always his when he stayed the night at Cordelia and Lawrence's house, Daniel's train of thought moved to the next day when his two young nieces sleeping across the landing would awake to the excitement of Christmas morning, and if they found him less than cheerful they would be disappointed. So smiles would be called for at breakfast-time and lots of fun.

CHAPTER SIX

THE SAME APPLIED to the children's ward, even more so for young ones in a strange environment away from all the things they were used to, and parents had been given extra visiting hours to make up for the change of circumstances so that they could bring some of the things that Santa and his reindeer had brought for them.

For any who had not received any toys, for whatever reason, the nurses, at Darcey's suggestion along with the hospital facilities, had brought toys and nice things for them, so that no child was missed out, and as she walked the short distance to the ward the next morning it felt more like a joy than a duty to be there for them.

She had put the happenings of the night before to the back of her mind until the day was over and the night was ready to unfold on her, except for the memory of her brother's phone call, which had brought back how it used to be with them, and to have that feeling again after the stresses she had endured before moving to Seahaven was relief untold. What she had faced before moving to Seahaven had helped to put the moments she'd spent in Daniel's arms into perspective.

When she arrived at the ward parents and friends were already arriving, and to give the day staff time to see that their young patients were washed and given their breakfast, followed by whatever medication had been prescribed for them, the hospital had provided breakfast for their families in one of its restaurants.

It was to be a short respite for them in the midst of their anxiety, and much as she had tried to put Daniel out of her mind Darcey couldn't help thinking that the day lacked his presence there just as much as she missed him.

Her return to her accommodation at the end of her working day was just as drab as she had visualised it would be. There was brightness all the way along the promenade but none where she lived, and as Darcey went inside it was there, the loneliness that she dreaded.

On a sudden impulse she showered and changed into evening clothes beneath a warm winter coat and set off along the seafront to find a restaurant that wasn't booked up for the occasion, and wasn't finding it easy when she saw Bridget and Ely coming towards her and there was no avoiding them.

'Hello, there,' the elderly boatman said. 'Surely you're not on your own on Christmas Day?'

'Yes, I'm afraid so,' she admitted uncomfortably.

'Then you must dine with us!' Bridget exclaimed. 'Everything is ready for our Christmas meal. We just came out for a breath of air, choosing to eat at home, and you are most welcome to join us, my dear.'

'I couldn't intrude like that,' Darcey protested weakly.

'You wouldn't be intruding,' Ely told her. 'Any friend of Daniel's is a friend of ours.'

'I am very interested in the Young Sailors' Club,' Darcey admitted. 'I would love to hear more about that.'

'So come and eat with us and we'll tell you all about it,' Bridget said.

'You are too young and bonny to be spending the evening of Christmas Day on your own. How have you passed the rest of it?'

'I'm Sister on the children's ward at Oceans House,' she told her, 'and I've been working there all day.'

'But Daniel wasn't, I take it,' Ely commented. 'He will have been with his sister's children. He loves those young ones. Pity he hasn't some of his own.'

And Darcey found herself thinking that she could do something about that if he would let her, but he would have to want to first.

Bridget and Ely lived in a neat fisherman's cottage not far from the harbour and made her most welcome in their small property where cooking smells lay on the night air and a log fire in the hearth took away the chill of the night outside, so that Darcey's loneliness disappeared as they answered all her questions about the Young Sailors' Club and Daniel himself, who they were obviously very fond of.

But Bridget was concerned that as well as his work at the hospital he was committed to turning out with the lifeboat when required, and although she made no comment Darcey agreed with her sentiments wholeheartedly.

There was no mention of the old lighthouse in the conversation. Clearly Daniel was intending that the repairs and renovation of it were to be a surprise and her amazement that he should have shared his secret dream with her surfaced again.

As the clock's hands began to move towards midnight she got up to go, with the thought of going back to Oceans House in the morning, and as she thanked them for their hospitality Ely said, 'I'll see you safely home, my dear.'

Bridget chipped in with, 'You are welcome any time, Darcey. It has been a pleasure to have you with us.' Tears pricked at their kindness and almost overflowed when the elderly lady went on to say, 'It is a shame that you are on duty tomorrow, or you could have gone sailing with Daniel and some of the young ones, it being Boxing Day.'

When she arrived back at her small residence and Ely had gone after seeing her safely inside, Darcey sank down by the window and, looking out into the Christmas night, gazed at the brightness of the stars and the moon above, while the kindness she had received from Ely and Bridget kept at bay the loneliness that she'd been dreading.

The only trouble with that was they would be sure to mention in Daniel's presence how they'd met her all alone on the promenade and he would want to know the reason why. But she would worry about that tomorrow, she decided, and with another day on the ward ahead put the thought of sailing with him to the back of her mind.

There might come another chance for that, she thought as sleep crept over her, and if it didn't happen she would always have the memory of the time he'd taken her to see the lighthouse.

It was good weather for sailing the next day. So much so that Daniel had taken one lot of the young would-be sailors out in the morning and another group in the afternoon as the sea was calm and the sky blue and cloudless, which made Darcey's absence even more disappointing, but he understood.

She'd been new to Seahaven and had probably thought he'd been in a rush to get to know her as she hadn't been aware of his reputation for steering clear of her sex, so he needed to slow down, give her some breathing space.

When Ely had mentioned casually how he and Bridget had met Darcey all alone on the evening of

Christmas Day he'd been horrified. Was he so unlikable that she'd lied when telling him that she was booked up for the Christmas period, and if so how was she going to get the days over?

He had his answer when he popped into the hospital to meet up with the elderly consultant covering for him over Christmas, a man who'd been his tutor when Daniel had been a student. As they chatted over coffee in the cafeteria, James Collins said, 'I was impressed with the children's ward on my first shift when I took over.'

'Yes,' Daniel agreed. 'Darcey Howard, the regular sister, has taken time off during the Christmas period and will be pleased to hear that the rest of the staff are how she would want them to be.'

The other man was looking at him in puzzlement. 'She has been there all the time ever since I arrived. I met her on my first morning on the wards, and even caught a glimpse of her as I was arriving this morning. It would seem there has been a change of plan perhaps.'

'Yes, maybe,' Daniel agreed, thinking grimly that he had his answer to where Darcey was hiding out over Christmas. Was he such a monster that she had to resort to that sort of thing to avoid him?

It was further proof of what Ely and Bridget had said. Darcey wasn't going anywhere other than Oceans House. Wasn't spending Christmas with anyone except the nursing staff, and had been so desperate to avoid him after what he'd said about Cordelia's matchmaking that she'd concocted a story about a busy social life to keep him at a distance, so he could imagine how welcome his kiss on the promenade on Christmas Eve had been.

But he had to see for himself that she was there, and the only way to do that was to visit the children's ward. So while the other man continued with his rounds Daniel made his way to the ground floor, where she would be if what he had just heard was correct…and it was.

Darcey was seated at the desk in the office, talking to the parents of one of her young patients, and he felt sick at the thought of how determined she'd been not to spend any time over Christmas with him.

The visitors were getting up to go and when she saw him observing her from the doorway of the ward he saw the colour drain from her face. But she didn't falter as she repeated the reassurances that she'd been able to give to the concerned parents about their child as they said their goodbyes.

Once they had gone he was beside her in a stride and, shutting the office door behind him, asked without preamble, 'So this is why you didn't want to come sailing with me, you would rather be here. I might applaud your self-sacrificing gesture if I didn't know that it was aimed at avoiding me.'

'I'm here because I told you a lie and then found I had to make it believable,' she told him tonelessly.

'I'm not with you,' he gritted. 'What has being

here to do with you not wanting to come sailing with me?'

'I'd already put my name down to work over Christmas because I dreaded how awful it would be if my days turned out to be as empty and lonely as my nights,' she told him in a low voice.

'When you asked me to go sailing with you I was already committed to working over the holiday and had to think of a reason to refuse the invitation so I pretended I was booked up over Christmas because I didn't want you to know how lonely I am most of the time and start pitying me.'

'And that was it!' he exclaimed.

'Yes, that was the reason why, pathetic as it is,' she admitted wearily.

'And to think that I convinced Cordelia that you were booked up for the whole of Christmas!' he said tightly, and then with his tone softening added, 'She and Lawrence are going to be partying again to-night and I know they would love to see you again. Suppose I pick you up when you've finished here and take you to their place? How soon could you be ready?'

Faster than the speed of light, she wanted to tell him, but instead said casually, 'About an hour after I leave here, which will give me time to shower and get changed into something appropriate.'

'Such as the lovely dress that you were wearing on Christmas Eve when we met on the promenade?'

'Er...no, not necessarily,' she told him. 'I've worn

it a couple of times now and I do have other clothes to choose from.' With her glance on the ward that awaited her presence, she said, 'Will you forgive me for lying to you, Daniel? I really did want to go sailing with you and the club.'

'Yes, of course,' he said gravely. 'Perhaps we could make up for that disappointment by driving out to the lighthouse sometime to view what the firm that I've commissioned to do the repairs has done so far.'

'I would love to!' she cried, and as he turned to go was unable to refrain from asking what was uppermost in her mind, and it didn't concern the lighthouse. 'Will you always be on call for the lifeboat?'

'Yes, I am totally committed. They need me,' he replied. 'Although I suppose there might come a time when someone else is willing to take my place, but until then I shall follow in my father's footsteps as long as the need is there.'

On that promise he went, with a last reminder that he would call for her as arranged once her commitment to the children in her care was finished for the day.

Darcey was ready when Daniel came for her in the evening but not exactly sparkling due to an extra-busy day on the ward without his brisk expertise. And she was having doubts about letting him foist her onto his sister and her husband after they had already made her so welcome on Christmas Eve.

But most of all at the back of her mind was his

reply to her question about his commitment to the lifeboat. She couldn't question it, understood totally. But would she want to spend the rest of her life in Seahaven praying for its safe return, that their children still had a father in the knowledge that the man she loved had only the bricks and mortar of an old lighthouse to remind him of his father?

Unaware of her fears on his behalf, Daniel's only concern on arriving was to reassure her regarding his intention to take her to his sister's once again, and when she mentioned her concerns on that score he just smiled and commented that Cordelia had mentioned she was looking forward to talking with her again, and that also there would be the chance for Darcey to chat further with the elder of his two young nieces about anything she wanted to know about nursing.

'Will that make you feel less of an outsider?' he asked, and Darcey swallowed hard at the thought that she must have sounded weak and whining when he'd come into the ward office that morning.

'Yes, hopefully,' she told him, and smiling at her reticence he brought the colour to her cheeks with his next comment, which was, 'Am I allowed to tell you that you look very beautiful?'

She was laughing now. 'Oh, yes, please do! I need something to boost my morale and I do like to wear black occasionally, although the dress isn't new.'

'It is to me, though,' he replied, and taking her hand he took her out into another Christmas night.

He drove her the short distance to his sister's house and hoped that nothing would go wrong in the evening ahead.

Daniel had been right about the young would-be nurse. No sooner had they arrived than Katie was ready to check their general health once they had been introduced to everyone there, and as Darcey watched him playing the part of the patient to the full there was an ache around her heart at the thought of how much he had missed by letting a stale marriage separate him from a family life of his own.

Daniel saw her expression and wondered what was causing her to look so solemn, but before he could ask, Cordelia came to chat while their friends watched football on television, and it was all relaxing until he saw tiredness fall on Darcey like a cloak as a reminder that hers had been a long day, with others to follow, and tenderness washed over him as they said goodbye to the only family he had with the thought uppermost that she had even less.

They had to pass the apartments where he lived on the way home, and glancing across at her sitting quietly beside him in the passenger seat Daniel said, 'I seem to be in and out of your place all the time, Darcey, but you have never seen mine. Are you too tired to come in for a coffee?'

She smiled across at him. 'No. I would like that. I imagine it is quite sumptuous.'

'I don't know about that,' he said laughingly. 'It is

more like an empty shell that I use to eat and sleep in, a boring place really.'

He was driving into the parking area, which was well lit, and Darcey became silent as the difference between their two residences became apparent, yet it stood to sense that it would, and did it matter? They were only socialising like this because it was Christmas.

She had already weighed up the pain threshold of loving him with the memory of losing her parents still starkly clear, and tonight was not going to be a stepping stone in that direction, she prayed as Daniel settled her into a comfortable sitting room while he went to make the coffee. When he came in with it, as if he'd read her thoughts he said, 'It is midnight, Darcey, and you are already exhausted after a busy day at Oceans House, so much as I would like your company for longer, once we've had the hot drink I'm going to take you home.'

If he'd told her the truth it would have been that he longed to carry her up the stairs and make love to her in his lonely bed, but that would be a poor show of caring about her tiredness, not how he wanted it to be at all, and short of offering her his guest room there was no way he could keep Darcey near until morning when she would require an early departure to get changed into her uniform, and might not thank him for that.

Darcey gazed at him above the rim of her coffee cup but said nothing, the memory of her fears of losing him to the sea feeling as if it would be a similar tragedy to that of her parents lost in the snows, and knowing that Daniel would always honour his father's devotion to the mighty ocean so near the town, no matter what. She could see nothing ahead but pain if he ever loved her as much as she was beginning to love him.

He was getting to his feet as she put her coffee cup down and he held out his hand. As she rose to face him he said quizzically, 'Can I take it that tonight you haven't been lonely?'

She flashed him a tired smile. 'You can indeed,' she said softly. 'I envy you your delightful family, Daniel.' Reaching forward, she stroked his face gently with her fingertips and said, 'Thank you for sharing them with me on this occasion.'

'It was a pleasure for all of us,' he said gravely, as if her tender touch wasn't making him long for more. 'And as for our young would-be nurse, don't be surprised if the next time you see me I'm covered in bandages and plasters.' Taking hold of her wrap, he draped it around her snugly and led her out into the night once more, where the warmth of the car awaited them.

When they got to her apartment Daniel saw her safely inside, and with Darcey's work routine as familiar as his own he didn't linger but had one last thing to say regarding her almost non-existent social life. 'I don't like to think of you alone on New Year's Eve,' he said sombrely.

'My two young nieces go to the birthday party of one of their friends on that occasion every year and stay overnight, which gives the rest of us—Cordelia, Lawrence and myself—the chance to go to the ball at the biggest hotel in town.

'This year I have a spare ticket that I got in case the doctor who is filling in for me at Oceans House would have liked to have gone, but he has another engagement for that night. So if you would like to join us you will be most welcome. I would pick you up at seven thirty.'

'Daniel, it is very kind of you to offer, but I'm afraid that I have something special planned for New Year's Eve,' she explained awkwardly, and cringed at his expression.

'Fine,' he said briskly, 'just as long as you won't be alone.' And during the short drive home he decided that maybe Darcey found him too overpowering, but if that was the case why didn't she say so?

Back at her apartment Darcey was going over those few embarrassing moments in her mind and cringing at the way she'd handled them. But she reasoned that, however much she would have liked to have gone to the ball with Daniel, her yearly pilgrimage to a church on New Year's Eve, wherever there might be one near, had to come first in remembrance of the deaths of her parents on that long-ago New Year's Eve, and during the week that followed the new closeness between the two of them that Christmas had brought seemed far away.

* * *

A nearby church was almost full when she got there on the night but she found a seat near the back and when she looked around her Darcey saw that Bridget and Ely were sitting nearby, and when they saw her and smiled across for a moment it was as if those she had lost were there in the friendly older couple.

Both were wearing winter coats, but as it was quite warm in the church they had unbuttoned them, and she could see that they were dressed in evening wear, which made her heart sink.

They must be going to the ball, she thought, and when they got there would be sure to tell Daniel that they had seen her elsewhere in the town, and a dampening thought was that if they were attending the church service first they must be confident that when it was over they would be in time for the ball.

But once Daniel had spoken to Bridget and Ely it would be too late for any afterthoughts on her behalf. It was an hour to midnight and Darcey was alone, as she had expected to be when she had refused Daniel's suggestion that she be his guest at the ball, but she had seen his friends since then and if they had met him earlier it hadn't sent him to her.

So maybe he'd had his fill of what he might see as her playing hard to get, as after seeing Bridget and Ely she was not likely to have gone to the ball without a ticket and risk being sent away if he didn't see her arrive.

The minutes were passing, soon it would be a

New Year, a time to make a fresh start for some, or make the best of what they had for others, and neither suggestion was appealing.

It was ten minutes to the hour when Darcey heard a car pull up outside the apartment and her mouth went dry. What now? she wondered, and as she opened the door to him she had her answer. There was no sweeping her into his arms, just questions needing answers.

'Why are you so secretive, for heaven's sake?' he asked as he stepped over the threshold, 'Or is it only with me that you are like that, such as hiding your loneliness from me when I was able to do something about it once I knew, and it was a joy to make you happy for a while.

'Yes, I have spoken to Bridget and Ely, and they told me that they saw you in church. What you did after that I have no idea, but when you said that you had something special that you had to do tonight, why didn't you say what it was so that I could have driven you there, or maybe even been present at the service where they saw you?'

'It was just something that I always do on New Year's Eve wherever I happen to be,' she told him, 'and it is a very private thing, Daniel, that is all. My parents lost their lives in an avalanche when they were skiing on New Year's Eve many years ago, and it was in their memory that I was unable to go to the ball with you.

'If I'd had the opportunity to check the time of everything properly I would have realised that I could have managed to get to both the church service and the ball, which I do so regret missing, but I wouldn't want to become a burden in your busy life because I'm new here in Seahaven,' she told him awkwardly.

He groaned inwardly at her enchanting honesty and thought she was one burden he would carry with him for ever if she would let him, and what could have been a more suitable occasion for them to get to know each other better than in the last hours of the old year and the first hours of the new one?

When Bridget and Ely had told him about seeing her in the church, he hadn't wanted to intrude into whatever need had taken her there until midnight was almost upon them, but he knew that he needed to be with her like he needed to breathe.

He held out his arms and, unable to help herself, Darcey moved into them, but the night was not to be theirs. A greater force than their attraction to each other had different plans for them as Daniel's phone rang, and as he listened to the voice at the other end his hold on her slackened.

'Yes, all right,' he said flatly. 'But I'll have to change first. I'm still in the clothes I wore to the ball and will change into the spare outfit that Ely keeps for me at his place. See you soon.' Disconnecting the call, he said, 'The lifeboat has been called out, Darcey. Some folks on a pleasure boat have come unstuck in the same place as where our young ones almost scuttled theirs not long ago.

'They've hired it for partying but have run into very high seas and the only one of them capable of bringing them safely back to shore has been drinking ever since they set off, so is totally out of it.' His hand was already on the door catch. 'Make sure that you lock up after me.' As an afterthought, he added, 'I'm due back on my usual routine at Oceans House in the morning, so I will see you then if all goes well with this callout.'

'And if it doesn't?' she questioned raggedly.

'It will, don't fret,' he informed her briskly, and was gone, and as she heard his car engine start up outside Darcey sank down onto the nearest chair and thought miserably that it could have turned out to be one of the most special moments of their lives, but if Daniel didn't return safely it would be the worst and she couldn't live the sort of life again where someone she loved was snatched away in a moment.

It might not have been so hard to cope with if he hadn't shown her the derelict lighthouse that he was having restored and told her the reason why.

At the time she had been moved by his acceptance of what must have been a terrible loss, but at that time she had been merely a sympathetic bystander, not a woman in love.

It was turning out to be a painful beginning to the first hours of the New Year, the two of them being on the brink of something magical that had fallen apart.

CHAPTER SEVEN

BRIDGET CALLED TO let Darcey know the lifeboat was out there, and after Darcey hung up, all she could think about was that when Bridget was gone, would *she* be expected to take the elderly woman's place, providing hot drinks and sandwiches for those who waited anxiously for the return of their loved ones?

No! She would want her life to be wrapped around children that she could love and adore with a fantastic father, but she was moving too fast. How could she be sure that it wasn't just a quick hug that Daniel had been about to bestow upon her? That saving lives on the sea came before even his expertise at Oceans House, and that love and marriage were a poor third after what had happened to his father.

The time was almost one o'clock in the early morning of New Year's Day and her main concern had to be with the sick and injured children who were in her care, Darcey thought as she lay sleepless beneath the covers, but at the back of her mind there were still Daniel's comments about her refusal to let him take her to the ball and the mix-up of the timing.

What else could go wrong? she questioned miserably, and turning her face into the pillow felt the dread from earlier return like a hand grasping her heart.

He had said on leaving that he would see her in the morning as he was back on schedule from then, and the thought of how she would cope if he didn't arrive was beyond thinking of. But there could be various other reasons that might delay him and with that frail comfort to hold onto she finally drifted off to sleep, until the alarm clock beside her bed awoke her to reality once more in a winter dawn with no phone calls to draw comfort from or messages of a safe undertaking on the mat. This could mean that the lifeboat was still out there, or that Daniel had got back and rather than disturb her had gone to bed knowing that they would be meeting up first thing in the morning.

Then again, there was a third possibility that had occurred to her when he'd received the phone call the night before. It was that of expecting her to be as easygoing about the danger involved as he was, and if that was the case he couldn't be more wrong.

There was no sign of him when she arrived on the children's ward, or anywhere else for that matter. No one had seen anything of him so far, which made everything that she'd felt so definite about seem unimportant.

His absence had to mean that the lifeboat was still out in dangerous waters, she thought frantically, and began her rounds with dogged purpose to stop herself from weeping, until magically she heard the voice that she longed to hear.

He was there, observing her from the doorway of the ward with dark hazel eyes red-rimmed, his face unshaven, and when he beckoned her she went to him as if in a trance.

'I've only just got back,' he said, 'so I'm going to have a shower in the en suite bathroom adjoining my office and then ask one of the hospital's restaurants to bring me some breakfast. Once all that has been accomplished, I will start my rounds, with the children's ward first as I usually do.'

As their glances held, Darcey thought there was no mention of what he and the rest of the lifeboat crew had been facing during the long hours of a stormy night and maybe it was just as well. She was concerned enough without a blow-by-blow account that would make the kind of life she dreamed of seem even less likely to ever be hers.

But for the present there was the exquisite relief of seeing Daniel back in familiar surroundings, and when he appeared later, looking scrubbed and clean and ready for action, she was content until he said, 'When are you due for a break after being on duty all over Christmas?'

'I've got a week off, starting tomorrow,' she said awkwardly, as they approached the first small bed in their line of vision.

'And have you anything planned?' he asked.

'No, not especially,' she told him. 'Why do you ask?'

'I'm intending going to see how the work on the lighthouse is coming along and thought you might like to join me for the day, as it isn't quite as isolated as it appears. Often in years gone by one would find a manor house and a cluster of cottages that housed the lighthouse keepers not far away from it, along with a small church. All of which are still there but no longer lived in, and I might decide to change all that by buying the manor house.'

Darcey was gazing at him in disbelief, but they had reached the bedside of Luke, a ten-year-old boy who stared at them unblinkingly and asked how long it would be before he could play football again after a serious leg injury. As she listened to Daniel explaining gently that it could be some time, but it would happen one day, Darcey knew beyond doubt that he was the man that she wanted to father any children she might have, and if he couldn't be for any reason she would do without.

As they moved on to the next bed their private lives were shelved to attend to the needs of their young patients, and by the time that was accomplished Darcey was due for her lunch break and Daniel would proceed to the adult wards that had still to be visited due to his late arrival.

'So what do you think of that for an idea, buying the manor house?' he said as they were about to separate. 'I've had it in mind for some time and would like your opinion.'

'Why me?' she croaked.

'Why do you think?' he said softly. 'I want you to be the mother of my children one day.'

'And that's it?' she questioned flatly. 'Expecting me to be the mother of a one-parent family if you don't come back from a lifeboat callout? I've endured that kind of thing for over ten years with Alexander after our parents went in a flash and left us alone, and I can't bear to make another commitment of that kind, Daniel.'

'Yes, of course, I understand,' he said levelly. 'But my father's sacrifice was a willing one, as my mother had already gone and Cordelia and I were adults in charge of our own lives.'

'And what would your decision be if you found yourself in a similar position to his?' she questioned.

'If I had a wife and children I would only risk my life in the most extreme circumstances, I can promise you that, but whether it would be enough is up to you, Darcey.'

'I don't know,' she said painfully. 'I just don't know. You haven't said that you love me, have you? Just that you would like me to have your children.'

He was observing her with a twisted smile. 'I've loved you ever since you let me put your luggage up on the rack in the train, though I don't know why as when I saw you on the ward the next day and saw how really beautiful you were I realised that you had been sad and exhausted, far from your best on the journey.'

'But I must go, Darcey, I'm way behind in my routine today after my late start. Do you think we could meet up again this evening and finish what we were discussing earlier?'

'Yes, I suppose so,' she told him weakly. 'Although I don't see what it can achieve. Our needs are too different, our lives too far apart. We work together. It's not a good idea for us to get involved.'

He was laughing. 'I'm not sure I would agree with that, so what about tonight? I'll take you for a meal, but do you want to change out of your uniform first?'

'Yes, it won't take long, about half an hour?' she said hesitantly.

'That's fine and, in the meantime, while you're getting ready I'll call briefly on Bridget and Ely as my being in America for the last two weeks meant them having to cope with the club members, who can be a handful at times.'

Turning towards the stairs that would take him to the floor above where adult patients were being treated, he said, 'I'll call for you half an hour after you finish, Darcey, and no need to dress up for such an occasion if the answer to my suggestion is going to be no.' And on that cheerful comment he left her to a brief lunch in the staff restaurant with the feeling that she was out of her depth, in love totally for the first time…and not coping.

Daniel had booked a table at a different restaurant from the one he'd taken her to the last time to avoid casting any more shadows than there were already in their relationship, and he could tell that Darcey read his mind.

'I suggest that we eat first and talk afterwards,' he said gently, and she nodded mutely.

The food was excellent but she ate it mechanically with no enjoyment and when the meal was over he looked around him and said, 'It's too crowded in here, Darcey, to be having a serious discussion amongst all these folks. There is no privacy and too many of them know who we are. We'll go to my place, if that's all right with you.' When she nodded once again he called the waiter over and settled the bill.

There was no conversation between them as Daniel drove the short distance to his apartment, or when they were inside for the first few moments, but when she took off the winter coat she was wearing and went to stand by the fire it came like a rushing wind, the chemistry between them, and when he held out his arms she went into them like a homing bird, with his every kiss a magical moment, but when at last they drew apart and he said softly, 'So can we start arranging a wedding?' he felt her withdrawal like a knife wound.

'I thought you'd brought me here to discuss both of our points of view,' she told him flatly, 'but it would seem that it is only yours that matters.' Before he could reply she had flung her coat on and was whizzing through the front door like a rocket, and by the time he had gathered his wits she was out of sight. He thought, so much for that, he'd made a mess of the whole thing.

He had meant what he'd said to be gentle teasing before telling her that since their discussion that morning he had been in touch with the authorities who were in charge of appointing the coxswains on the lifeboats and would have to await their decision with regard to his request.

Obviously he should have told Darcey that first, instead of mentioning marriage and teasing her about a wedding, as if that was all he was bothered about. But her reaction to what he'd said had been so abrupt that he'd been taken aback, otherwise he would have gone on to tell her that he had wasted no time since that morning in considering her needs, and now there was no sign of her on the road outside.

Yet there was no way he was going to leave it at that so he drove onto the promenade, his concern increasing until he saw a taxi that she must have flagged down pulling away from the front of her apartment and went weak with relief. Not wanting to cause any further upsets, he drove back home the way he had come in sombre mood and it didn't lighten at all when only seconds after his return a frantic Cordelia phoned to say that his younger niece had suffered a spinal injury in an accident and was being transferred by ambulance straight to Oceans House so could he meet them there? He was on his way almost before she'd finished speaking.

* * *

When he got there the ambulance was just pulling up in the space provided for such vehicles and as Bethany was carried out on a stretcher, with the rest of her family close behind, Daniel thought grimly that this was the punishment he deserved for his thoughtless treatment of Darcey. As if she'd read his mind, she appeared beside him, having seen the ambulance arrive and witnessed his grave concern from the window of her apartment.

'What's wrong, Daniel?' she asked anxiously.

'I don't know until we get her inside,' he said bleakly. 'From what Cordelia said when she phoned, it sounds as if Bethany has had some sort of accident and it has affected her spine.'

'Oh, no!' she exclaimed. 'Poor little one! Can I do anything to help? I'm sorry for my outburst earlier. It was just that—'

'It's all right,' he said levelly as his young niece was lifted carefully out of the confines of the ambulance. 'Save it for another time, Darcey, if there ever is one.'

As Cordelia and her family followed the stretcher he stepped forward to greet them and, feeling unwanted and in the way, Darcey moved to one side and waited to see if he would take her up on her offer of help as there would be night staff to assist if he needed them.

'So put me in the picture,' Daniel said to Lawrence as the two men strode beside the hospital trolley with Bethany's sister Katie holding the sedated young patient's hand. With her arm supporting her friend in the rear, Darcey listened patiently as Cordelia explained tearfully what had caused the accident that had injured their daughter.

'We were going skiing at half-term,' she said, 'and had gone late night shopping for suitable clothes in one of the big stores when Bethany lost her footing at the bottom of an escalator and fell backwards onto the metal steps. She was screaming with pain as we lifted her off and unable to stand, so the store sent for an ambulance, which brought us straight here to Daniel.

'When I rang to tell him what had happened he'd just got in from somewhere and didn't sound very happy, but when I told him about the accident he was back in the car and wasted no time in meeting the ambulance on its arrival, as you saw.'

'He will be sending Bethany for X-rays first,' Darcey reminded her, 'so that he can assess the damage to her back, and your family will need you near, Cordelia. So if you go ahead with the two men, I'll wait here as I don't feel Daniel will want me around unless he has a use for me, which is not likely.'

If her friend had been less traumatised she would have wanted to know what was meant by that cryptic comment, but with all that she had on her mind taking first place she hurried off and Darcey was left to wait until there was a result from the X-rays before any further communication with the man who she thought achingly loved the lifeboat more than he loved her.

Why hadn't Darcey stayed with Cordelia? Daniel wondered as he waited for the X-rays. If she didn't want anything to do with him any more, so be it, but why take it out on his sister, especially in her hour of need? They were his family and he would move heaven and earth to save them pain if he could. His venture into romance had been a step too far, it seemed, if Darcey didn't want to be in the same room as him.

But the X-rays were ready for his scrutiny, and as he studied them relief washed over him in a thankful tide.

There was severe bruising and bleeding of his little niece's back but no spinal damage or broken bones. With gentle nursing while in Darcey's care, and his expertise available at a moment's notice, she should make a full recovery.

When he looked up to where the little one's loving parents were waiting to hear what could have been so much worse, Daniel was smiling as he said, 'No broken bones, just a lot of soreness that will disappear with tender care. But no skiing at half-term, I'm afraid, and I would recommend a few days in the children's ward with Darcey in charge, just to make sure that our small patient is progressing satisfactorily.' As he gazed at those he loved, there was just one person missing, but what was new about that?

'I must go and tell her,' Cordelia said as if she'd

read his mind. 'I wanted her to be with us when you gave us the verdict, whether it was good or bad, but she seemed to feel that she would be intruding and said she'd wait in the corridor.'

'Go and tell her by all means,' he agreed, 'and when Darcey joins us I will confirm what I said about having Bethany stay here for the next few days, where Darcey will be in charge. There is no one better.

'Lawrence and you will be able to visit for as long as you like as there aren't any restrictions, and I will be around to keep my professional eye on things, so please feel free to explain that to Darcey when you see her.' As she listened to his instructions, Cordelia wondered what had gone wrong between them.

When she found Darcey still waiting in the corridor, her friend asked worriedly, 'Have the X rays come through?'

'Yes, thank goodness,' was the reply. 'There is bruising but no broken bones and Daniel wants Bethany to stay in the children's ward for a few days, or as long as it takes for her to recover. He is not pleased that you weren't there when he announced the results.'

'Yes, it would seem that he and I are not as compatible as we thought,' Darcey said flatly as they went to join the others.

Daniel was on the phone to the night sister when they appeared, explaining that they would be bringing another small patient to the children's ward in a few moments and that he was going to stay there for the time being to watch over her during the night.

'I've persuaded Lawrence to take you and Katie home once Bethany is settled in there,' he told Cordelia when he'd finished the call, 'and I will be in touch immediately if there are any further problems.' And with his glance on Darcey, who so far hadn't spoken, he continued, 'I shall stay until you arrive in the morning, and when I've left will expect to be informed at the slightest sign of anything you are concerned about.'

'Yes, of course,' she said levelly, and wished he wouldn't speak to her as if she was a stranger.

Even worse, she was being dismissed as he said, 'And now I suggest you get some sleep, knowing that I shall be with Bethany until you take over at eight o'clock tomorrow.' After that pronouncement he turned and held Cordelia close and at the same time put his arm around Lawrence's shoulders while a tearful Katie snuggled close, telling them gently to go home and rest and he would be in touch in the morning.

When he turned to say goodnight to Darcey she'd gone, hurt that Daniel could change so quickly when she loved him so, but a sweet little girl who had slipped on hard metal and hurt her back was going to be her first concern in days to come, not whether anything was left of their brief relationship.

Seated beside Bethany's bed in the children's ward, Daniel watched over his little niece with ragged calm, alert to every sound or movement that she made in spite of the medication she'd been given at the time of the accident, and when he wasn't reliving the moment of Cordelia's horrifying phone call he was remembering Darcey's hurt and anger at his suggestion regarding a wedding when he hadn't told her about him having already asked for someone to take his place on the lifeboat.

The magic of those moments before she'd flung herself out into the night in hurt and anger had gone, and if he were to tell her now about his request for someone to take his place on the lifeboat it would seem as if it was a quick afterthought and he was no lover of that sort of thing. So he needed to let it lie for a while. Maybe until Darcey had seen the manor house near where his father's memorial was going to be.

Yet knowing her, she would be happy in one of the cottages that had previously housed the lighthouse keepers if she knew that he really loved her, let alone the manor house, and that was the problem. How was he going to convince her of that?

If he told Ely what he was proposing to do, he knew the man would be grieved to see him go and so would Bridget, but hopefully they would understand, and there was no doubt about what Cordelia would say as all she had ever wanted was for him to be happy. It was when it came to his own feelings that he faltered.

In Darcey he had found the love of his life, but she

was hurt and bruised by what life had done to her so far, and he didn't want her to be hurt even more because of him.

There was a little cry of pain from Bethany and when she opened her eyes and saw him sitting there, a big tear rolled down her cheek as she said, 'I fell and hurt my back, didn't I, Uncle Daniel?'

'Yes, you did, my little love,' he said softly, 'and I'm here to watch over you and make sure you get better very soon.' He smiled as he gazed at her. 'Would you like a drink and something to eat?'

'Can I have an ice-cream cone?' she asked weakly. 'My mouth is very dry.'

'Yes. I'll ask one of the nurses to bring one from the café upstairs, which is the only place open at this time where they have that sort of thing. But you will have to let me hold it while you lick it because of your sore back. OK?'

'Yes, please,' she said, and he wondered if he had botched his chances of being a father to children of his own by upsetting Darcey like he had. Would she want to be left alone after the evening's earlier catastrophic mix-up? But the ice cream was on its way for his niece and he had a job to do.

Once the treat had been enjoyed to the full, Daniel checked her temperature and was relieved to find it normal, and when two of the nurses on his instructions had gently turned his little niece onto her side he was able to inspect the damage to her back, which, although sore in parts, he knew could have been much worse, and by the time a fresh application of a soothing ointment had been applied again, Bethany had gone back to sleep.

CHAPTER EIGHT

IT WAS TWO O'CLOCK in the morning and Darcey was sleepless because the happenings of the evening were too fragile and hurtful to be put out of her mind.

First there had been Daniel's marriage proposal that had sent her back home like a rocket because there had been no mention of her fear of the sea claiming him as it had his father, and when later they'd met up at the hospital and she'd apologised for leaving so abruptly earlier in the evening, he had been the one who had indicated that the subject was closed.

With Cordelia and Lawrence totally distraught, Daniel had persuaded them to go home for a few hours while he watched over their daughter, and hadn't even noticed when she had gone home to rest, to be ready for the coming morning in the children's ward, where she and her staff would take over when Daniel took a break from his loving vigil.

It was all logical thinking but not sleep-producing, she thought. Even as it registered, she was dressing quickly and hurrying out into the night to the hospital.

'Darcey!' he exclaimed tonelessly as she appeared in the dimly lit ward. 'What are you doing here? Go back to bed.'

'I came to see how Bethany is,' she told him, 'and to ask if you would like me to bring you something from the restaurant.'

'No, thanks, I'm fine,' was the reply. 'The nurses are keeping me fed and watered.'

Looking down at the sleeping child, she asked softly, 'And what about your small patient? How is she?'

'At this moment content,' he said levelly, 'having just had an ice cream and the dressing on the soreness of her back dealt with, but once all that wears off she will still be in a lot of pain, which is why you should be bedded down for the night instead of here.'

'Yes, maybe I should,' she agreed, aware that it was the day she was due to go on leave and was now not intending to do any such thing until Bethany's condition had improved.

Cordelia and Lawrence had been kindness itself to her over the lonely days of Christmas. The least she could do in return was to be there for them at such a time, and as for her replacement, the staff nurse who was to have covered her role for the coming week would be happy to be relieved of the responsibility as she was heavily pregnant. Without further comment, Darcey went, with the hurtful thought in mind that Daniel's passion had been short-lived.

Daniel groaned softly when she'd gone, having

wanted to hold her close and tell her how much she meant to him, but the day's happenings had taken their toll. His concern for his small niece had to come first, and as if the thought had transferred itself to her, she awoke, began to cry, and it was a case of another gentle application of the soothing ointment and a cool drink before she went back to sleep.

Back at the apartment Darcey was doing what she'd been told to do, settling down for what was left of the night, but it wasn't to sleep, she thought bleakly. Daniel was very much mistaken if he thought she could switch off the nightmare happenings of a day that would soon be drawing to a close unresolved.

For one thing, she was most concerned on Cordelia and Lawrence's behalf that a shopping trip should end in their small daughter being hospitalised, but Daniel being who he was had been there for them, so at least one of the day's catastrophes had not gone unattended, and as for the other, the rapture it had also brought with it had disappeared.

He had said that he wanted her to be the mother of his children, and as she'd watched him with his small niece she'd thought there were two sides to that. Children needed a father too and he would have been all that she could wish for them when the time came, but the give and take would have had to be equal, not all on her side, although now it didn't matter. The divide that had appeared between them was too big to be treated as a lovers' tiff.

* * *

It was only after Darcey had returned to her apartment to obey his instructions that Daniel had remembered that she was due for time off during the week to come, after being on duty all through the Christmas period, and he had just messed it up again, as if his needs came first. But why hadn't she reminded him, for heaven's sake?

The problem of Bethany's care would have to be resolved like that of the other young patients after he had apologised and transferred his instructions to whoever would be taking her place, and then maybe the two of them could allow themselves a fresh start to their relationship.

But he wasn't relishing having to account for another misunderstanding after omitting to tell Darcey that he had wasted no time in trying to find a replacement to take on his lifeboat duties.

When she appeared later, looking heavy-eyed and pale, he was quick to apologise for his memory lapse. 'I'm so sorry for making my demands of you last night with regard to you taking Bethany under your wing during working hours,' he said, 'as that doesn't apply to the coming week, does it? You are on leave and that is how it must stay after all the time you put in during the Christmas break.' With a glance at the sleeping child, he added, 'The person who is due to take your place will manage very nicely, I'm sure, and what is more Cordelia and her family are here.

They arrived at six o'clock and have gone up to the restaurant to have a quick bite before I leave them to it, as I have a very busy day ahead in Theatre and on the wards.'

'Which makes me all the more intent on being here,' she told him. 'They are good friends and have shown me much kindness during my solitary existence over Christmas.' She gently reached out a hand and stroked Bethany's hair before saying, 'I will need to know your wishes regarding Bethany's treatment before you sign off. And, Daniel, with regard to us, maybe we were too hasty in allowing a commitment to form between us that we are not capable of fulfilling.'

'So that is what you think, is it?' he said with steely calm, restraining the urge to demonstrate how mistaken she was about that. Collecting the paperwork that he had been working on during the night as his young charge had slept, he passed her the sheet on top and said, 'Those are my instructions regarding Bethany's treatment. If you have any problems, you will find me somewhere in the building.'

Then he had gone and she did so wish that he hadn't. When his sister and her family appeared some seconds later Cordelia exclaimed, 'Darcey! We thought you were due for some time off? This can't be right.'

'It is very right indeed that I of all people should be here for my friends and their hurt little one,' she said gently. 'I had nothing planned for the coming week and if I had I would have cancelled it. Daniel has given me all the details for Bethany's treatment and her progress so far before he went to start on his usual Monday morning clinic, with instructions to seek him out immediately if the need arose.' She sent a smile in Katie's direction. 'When you come next time, bring your nurse's outfit and you can help us on the ward.' She was rewarded with a cry of delight.

At that moment Bethany awoke and as Cordelia helped her daughter eat, Darcey went to check on the rest of her young patients and wished that Daniel was there, doing his rounds with her as he would normally be, while instead his presence had been restricted to the night hours that were going to be followed by a very busy day.

Yet typically he managed to call at the ward for a few moments in the lunch hour and was satisfied to hear that the soreness of Bethany's lower spine was decreasing, she was in less pain and that a second X-ray had shown no further complications.

'When will we be able to take her home?' Lawrence asked, while Cordelia plied her brother with a sandwich and a mug of tea and Darcey stood by silently.

'In a few days, I would think,' Daniel told him, and with his glance on her continued, 'But I don't want to rush it as I did with something a few days ago that went all haywire.' He got to his feet, ready to depart, and she knew that she didn't want him out of her life ever, no matter what happened.

* * *

By Friday Bethany was well enough to go home. The damage to her back was healing well. She was able to walk slowly around the ward, getting to know some of the other children, and when Cordelia and Lawrence came for her she was almost reluctant to leave, but the thought of being able to play with Katie again and sleep in her own bed sorted that problem.

Daniel had been to see his small patient on her last morning in the children's ward and as Darcey watched them together it was there, as if only said a moment ago, that she was the one he wanted to give him children, which she would have been so happy to do, if only he had been equally willing to calm her fears regarding his commitment to the lifeboat, because there was always the memory of how she and Alex had been left young and parentless amongst the snows that day.

He appeared at her side when she was having a coffee and a sandwich in the staff restaurant during the lunch hour and asked, 'Have you sorted out the free time that I denied you when Bethany was brought in?'

'Yes,' she told him levelly. 'I'm having next week off. I haven't planned anything so far, but thought I might go and see Alex for a few days.' Alex had emailed to let her know he'd run out of money, so had come home and was staying with friends. He was working in a bar to get enough money to go travelling again. 'It will mean staying in a hotel somewhere near where he's staying, but as long as he's around so that we can meet during any free time he has, it will be fine.'

'So he's home, then,' he commented. 'When did he get back?' Without waiting for an answer, he commented, 'I could drive you there if you want. If you recall, the trains were very busy on the day we found ourselves going in the same direction and to the same place.'

'Oh, yes.' She recalled it all right, Darcey thought weakly, and to be next to him for a couple of hours in the closeness of the car in the present circumstances, which had arisen only a week ago when Daniel had wanted her to marry him, would be an ordeal she didn't want to have to face.

'I shall make sure that I don't travel in the rush hour,' she said hurriedly, 'but thanks for the offer.' And with a complete change of subject that came from her love for him, and knowing how much he achieved with regard to the burden of care for others that he coped with all the time, she asked, 'Have you had time for some lunch?'

'No,' he said, 'but I'm going to do something about that in the next few moments.' As she arose hurriedly, her lunch break at an end, he wished that someone, somewhere would want to take over from him on the lifeboat. In the meantime, he was hoping that the lighthouse he had bought in memory of his father would soon be ready to be unveiled for all to see.

* * *

When Darcey phoned her brother to say that she intended to pay him a short visit during the coming weekend he was highly pleased. 'I've missed you,' he said. 'It was fabulous while we were away but no one will ever take your place, big sister. Shall I book you in somewhere?'

'Yes, please,' she told him. 'From Friday morning to Sunday evening somewhere close to you.'

'Will do,' he'd promised buoyantly. 'I'll ring back as soon as I have that sorted, and if I'm not working when your train is due, I'll meet you at the station.'

When they'd finished chatting Darcey sat back and gave some thought to how she was going to occupy herself for the rest of the week, and a vision of the derelict lighthouse came to mind. She had never seen it since the day that Daniel had taken her there when she'd viewed it in its dilapidated condition.

Now from what Bridget and Ely had told her when she'd dined with them on Christmas Day, the alterations were almost complete. Soon there would be a public dedication of Daniel's tribute to his father, and with the burden of their quarrel about the lifeboat raw and hurting she did not intend to attend that occasion.

But in her free time during the coming week there was nothing to stop her from visiting the scene on her own while he was occupied at Oceans House, she thought, and the following day she caught the promenade tram as far as it went in that direction and walked the rest of the way beneath a wintry sun until the lighthouse, resplendent in a fresh coat of white paint, came into view, with the words *In Memory of Mark Osbourne* on a brass plaque fitted centrally.

There were still workmen present and one of them stopped next to her and said, 'You are the sister from the children's ward at Oceans House, aren't you?

'Our little boy was in there a few weeks ago after a bad fall off his bike, but he's all right now.'

Darcey managed a weak smile, knowing the fact that she'd been seen at the site of the lighthouse renovation was sure to be mentioned to Daniel the next time he came there, and he would want to know the whys and wherefores of her visit.

But she would explain all that when the time came, and in the meantime the light of the winter afternoon was fading and the tram that had brought her there would be arriving soon to take her back, along with the bulk of the workforce, but she had yet to see the empty manor house and the other unoccupied properties that Daniel had described to her, which were vaguely visible on the horizon a mile or so away.

So, pointing herself in that direction, she walked briskly towards them, and the moment she was level Darcey understood Daniel's yearning to do two things, live in a house within sight of the memorial he had chosen for his father, and bring life back to the remote yet amazingly beautiful village where he had wanted to bring up their children when they arrived. But could she live with the thought always there that she might lose him to the sea, as she had lost her parents to the snow, and if he didn't understand her reasoning, could they have a happy life together?

Lost in her musings, she turned to make her way back to the lighthouse and was horrified to see the tram disappearing into the distance with not a soul in sight as it transported the workforce home on their last journey of the day.

Within minutes the winter dark fell on the empty houses behind her and with it came heavy rain, slashing against doors and windows as she ran from one to the next, desperate to find shelter. Until the heavy oak door of the manor house swung back on creaking hinges and she moved slowly into its unexpected shelter.

The most sensible thing would be to stay there until the rain cleared, she told herself, and then set off in the dark on the long walk back to her apartment, being careful to stay clear of the cliff edge where the lighthouse stood.

A depressing thought was that she wasn't going to be missed as no one at the hospital knew where she had set off to, and as she was on leave, neither Daniel nor Cordelia and Lawrence would expect her to do something as crazy as getting lost and having to shelter in a big empty house before starting on the long walk back to Seahaven in the dark.

It seemed that her phone wasn't working in the isolated place that she found herself in, and along with panic came the thought that there was someone who might have noticed that she was missing from the tram on its last journey of the day.

The man whose young boy had once been in Oceans House for treatment might have realised that she was not to be seen on its return journey and act accordingly.

It had been a really busy day and Daniel was on the point of leaving the hospital when one of the men he was employing to work on the lighthouse appeared and asked if he could spare a moment. Hoping that it would be something minor, Daniel took him into his office and waited to hear what he had to say. Surprisingly, it wasn't about work.

'I might be fussing about nothing,' his unexpected visitor told him, 'but felt I had to tell you that the sister on the children's ward here must have been off duty today and came to view the progress of the lighthouse renovation.' As Daniel observed him in amazement he went on to say, 'We chatted for a few moments and then she wandered off in the direction of the manor house and the other empty properties not far away, and when the last tram of the day came and we all piled on it, I didn't notice that she wasn't there until it had reached the promenade, and I felt that I must mention it as the weather up there left a lot to be desired.'

'You felt right,' Daniel told him with a sick feeling inside. He was already on his feet, reaching for his top coat, and asked, 'So there wasn't anyone there who might have given Darcey a lift home by car at all?' The other man shook his head. 'No. Sometimes we get the occasional motorist curious to see what is going on but not today, and the rest of us use the tram all the time.'

'Thanks for taking the trouble to let me know,' Daniel told him, tense and tight-lipped at the thought of Darcey lost in the dark of a winter night. If she'd gone to view the manor house after him mentioning it, he would be to blame if Darcey was lost out there in the cold, he told himself grimly, and when he saw the whiteness of the newly painted lighthouse at the top of the cliffs he leapt from the car in the hope that for once the workmen might have left it unlocked to provide some sort of shelter, but all was in order, there was nothing to make one want to linger there.

With his anxiety peaking, he took a lantern out of the car boot and once it was lit headed swiftly towards what had once been a thriving small village and was now dark, still and unlived in, but not as empty as he'd thought it would be if Darcey was lost in there.

The rain had stopped and in what was now a clear sky the moon shone down onto the place where Darcey had been sheltering, cold and lost for what had seemed like a lifetime, and she was now about to leave for the long walk back to civilisation, until she heard a twig snap under someone's foot not far away. The door swung back slowly to reveal the one person she had longed to be with in the dark silence that lay all around her.

'Daniel!' she sobbed, as tears of relief ran down her cold cheeks. 'I was praying that the workman that I'd chatted with earlier had noticed that I wasn't on the tram!'

He was taking his warm winter coat off with all speed and wrapping it around her, and only when she was snugly inside it he said softly, 'Your prayer was answered, but only when he was back home and stopped off at the hospital to inform me of his concern about you. I have to say I was amazed as after our last misunderstanding I would have thought that the lighthouse and the manor house that I'd thought of buying would have been the last two places you would want to visit on a free afternoon in doubtful weather.

'Having seen it in this condition, I imagine that your doubts regarding it must have multiplied, but I need to get you back to the car where the heater is, and I've got a flask of coffee that I coaxed out of the hospital snack bar before I left.' Giving Darcey the lantern to hold, he swung her up into his arms and carried her carefully back to the car.

Once inside he kissed her gently and said, 'Don't ever scare me like that again, no matter what our disagreements are.' And out came the flask with the coffee, and the car heater was serving its purpose delightfully, but she wanted to weep because nothing had changed regarding their different points of view about the lifeboat but she loved him too much to ever contemplate life without him.

For his part, Daniel was overwhelmed with regret for not making it clear to Darcey that he had done as promised and asked that another coxswain should be found to replace him on the lifeboat.

If Cordelia knew he was on the point of finding true happiness with Darcey and was hesitating, she would think he was crazy, but so far no one had come forward and he didn't want her to think that she meant so little to him that he wasn't bothering.

When they reached the promenade and her apartment was in sight he said, 'I think you should come to my place for the night. It will be warm in there and I can make you a meal and be there in case you suffer any side-effects from your ordeal.' But she shook her head.

'No, thanks just the same,' she told him, and getting out of the car she took off his coat and passed it to him.

His patience faltered. 'Fine, suit yourself!' he said in clipped tones. 'You know where I am if you need me.' And he drove off into the night.

When he arrived home there was a message from Cordelia to say that she hadn't seen Darcey for a while and was she all right? So before settling down for what was left of the evening he returned the call and explained that he had just left her, having driven her home from getting lost in a strange place that she'd been exploring because she was due some free time from the hospital.

'What a shame that you weren't both off together!' she exclaimed, ever hopeful, and left him to the solitude that once had been enough and now was the last thing he needed.

There was a note on his desk in a sealed envelope from Darcey the next morning. Brief and to the point, it said that she wished to apologise for her lack of gratitude for his kindness in bringing her home safely after her foolishness in getting lost like she had, and it went on to explain that she wouldn't be around for the next few days as she was going to see her brother while she had the opportunity.

Daniel groaned when he'd read it. First, because he wanted her in his arms, not a brief message on paper, and, second, much as he understood Darcey's need to see her brother, his days were going to be long without her being near.

Cordelia was due in with Bethany for another X-ray during the morning, hopefully the last, and if all went well she would be able to go back to school after the weekend with the damage to her back having healed satisfactorily. If that was the case, her older sister was also going to be denied the wearing of her nurse's uniform at every opportunity, unless another small patient appeared from out of nowhere.

There had still been no further callouts for the lifeboat, which was unusual for the time of year, and Daniel was hoping that it would stay that way until a replacement was found to fill his position, and once that was sorted the way ahead should be clear if Darcey loved him as much as he loved her, but until his place was filled there was no way he could betray his father's trust.

If Cordelia knew the situation he was in, she would be sure to say that their father would understand and would want him to be happy, but he had no intention of bringing his sister into the confusion of his thoughts. When he had given Bethany a clean bill of health he sent mother and child happily on their way without mentioning his own problems.

He had never shirked a callout for the lifeboat. It was as natural as breathing to all of them to risk their lives, along with himself whose father's name was revered amongst sea folk and many others besides.

But knowing how Darcey had lost her parents and taken on the heartbreaking task of caring for her young brother for many years, he understood her fear of the fates taking him from her with the kind of loss she had endured, and he couldn't let her live with that sort of dread always present if she married him.

CHAPTER NINE

WHEN THE TRAIN pulled into the station of her home town, Alex was waiting and Darcey's spirits lifted at the sight of him. He looked happy and relaxed and greeted her with a big smile of welcome.

As they walked the short distance to the small hotel where he had made her a reservation he had lots of questions to ask about Seahaven at the first opportunity.

That night, as the two of them sat in the hotel lounge after the evening meal, Alex said, 'I'm keen to see where you live and work, Darcey, in this place that is so near the sea, and I thought of visiting you over Easter, which isn't so far away. Would that be all right?'

'It would be lovely,' she said happily. 'Just as long as you wouldn't mind if I have to work the odd day or so if the ward is extra-busy. My place is very small and on hospital premises unfortunately, but I will find you somewhere nice to stay.'

'I don't mind where it is,' he said, 'and if some days you aren't around there will be plenty for me to explore in what sounds like a super place to live, with the sea top of the list.'

'Right,' she agreed, omitting to mention that it wasn't the top of her list at the moment, and told him, 'Let me know how long you want to come for and I'll make a booking for you somewhere. It will be just the two of us,' she said, happy at the thought of Alex for company when she was so miserable and lonely. She ached to have Daniel's arms around her, longed for him to find someone who would take his place on the lifeboat, but he hadn't mentioned it since their serious disagreement, which had to mean that he wasn't prepared to bend to her wishes.

But for the rest of the weekend she put those sorts of thoughts to the back of her mind, enjoying her time with Alex, and it wasn't until she was on the last train of the day in the dark night that was ending her short stay with Alex that Darcey allowed herself to think of the only man she would ever love. Amazingly, as if he'd read her mind Daniel was on the platform when she arrived back in Seahaven, his keen gaze scrutinising the faces of those for whom it was journey's end, and in seconds he was by her side, taking charge of her weekend case and smiling at her surprise.

'It's just a guess, my being here,' he told her. 'I was passing your apartment, saw that it was all in darkness, so decided to meet the last three trains of the day in case you were on one of them, as always at this hour the last tram has gone and taxis are in big demand.'

'Thank you for that,' she said awkwardly, as her hopes of good news about him having found a replacement for himself on the lifeboat didn't seem to be on his agenda, and she thought that it was as if she had asked him to do more than his love for her was capable of.

As they walked to where his car was parked he knew what she was thinking and could have explained that it wasn't for the want of trying. But so far no one had been found to replace him and, not having explained the situation to her in his first instance, he was torn between his love for her and his care for those whose lives were in peril.

When they reached her apartment and he was ready to drive off, Darcey didn't want him to go. She needed his arms around her, his kisses to set her on fire, yet didn't feel she could be as cruel as to ask those things of Daniel and not understand where his commitments had been before they'd met.

Yet she'd had responsibilities too, years of living with just Alexander in a much smaller house, and making sure that the love he had been denied by the deaths of their parents was always there, coming from her instead of them.

As she put her key in the lock he was ready to go and said briefly, 'Do I take it that you are back on the ward tomorrow?'

'Yes, you do, and I'm looking forward to it,' she said with a wry smile.

'I'll see you then,' he told her, and was gone.

'I don't remember thanking you for coming to meet me last night,' Darcey said the next morning on the ward. 'It was very kind.'

Kind! Daniel thought grimly, and fought back the urge to tell her that it was longing that had brought him to meet her at close on midnight, and a need to see for himself that she was back safely from just the few days when she had been out of his sight.

He'd been hoping that she wouldn't ask if he'd found himself a replacement to leave him free of his commitment to the lifeboat and she hadn't, which in its way was worse than if she had as it made the huge obstacle that separated them seem even more insurmountable than ever.

But there were young ones needing him with hurt and aching bodies, just like his young niece had been, and with Darcey beside him Daniel went from bed to bed, doing what he did best, and wondering whether he would ever have a child of his own.

As she watched Daniel talk to his small patients, Darcey's heart melted with tenderness, but it didn't wipe away the fear of being left totally alone this time as Alex didn't need his big sister any more, and she could tell just how reluctant Daniel was to leave the crew of the lifeboat, especially with the memorial to his father about to be revealed. In fact, she doubted whether he had even mentioned a replacement to anyone, and why should he if sea rescue meant more to him than she did?

When they'd finished the ward round and he had gone to the next group of patients needing his orthopaedic skills, Darcey looked around her and pondered if staying the course was the lesser of two hurts or not, or would it be better to make a clean break away from the situation in which she found herself. But what then?

Live the rest of her life in a cocoon of sadness away from the man she loved because she wanted him for herself, instead of having to share him with an assortment of risk-takers who thought they had the perilous sea under control and found they didn't?

At that moment a hospital porter appeared with a little girl called Bonnie, who had just been admitted, and all other thoughts were shelved in the needs of their newest patient.

Having had no time for food shopping since her late return from her weekend with Alex, Darcey went to the nearest of the promenade restaurants at the end of her working day, expecting nothing more than some hot food and a chance to unwind after the usual stresses of the ward, but found Brendan Stokes back in the area after a secondment at a hospital similar to Oceans House.

He was seated at a table for two, and pointing to the empty place opposite asked, 'Not with the boss or anybody, are you?' And Darcey thought grimly that he hadn't lost his unique brand of charm.

'No,' she told him. 'I'm going to get a sandwich from the restaurant's take-away counter as I intend to have an early night.' Without giving him the chance to comment further, she pointed herself in that direction and said goodbye to eating somewhere warm and cheerful.

Back inside her small residence, with the dark night closing in, she found a printed poster on the mat, announcing that the reopening and dedication of the lighthouse in memory of Daniel's father was to be on the coming Saturday, and on a slip of paper attached he had written:

I don't expect you to be there for various reasons, Darcey. One being your nasty experience not long ago when you were lost in that area, and another your aversion to all matters of this kind, but it would help to know that you are there in spirit on Saturday.

Love, Daniel

She would be there in more than just spirit, she thought tearfully. Her dread of more loneliness wasn't Daniel's fault, and as it seemed he wasn't prepared to pursue her plea of retiring from his position on the lifeboat, the future was going to be an empty thing no matter what.

* * *

The next morning when they were about to start the usual ward rounds she said to Daniel, 'I will be thinking of you on Saturday. Your father must have been a very special man, from what you say. What of your mother when she was alive, how did she cope with the constant fear of losing him?'

'With difficulty, like any other woman who loves a man who cares about the lives of others,' he said sombrely, and went on to say, 'I called to see Cordelia and Lawrence last night to inform them about Saturday's event before it became common knowledge, and she was so happy to know that our father is never going to be forgotten in this place and many others.' Then, as if he felt he had said enough on the subject, Daniel indicated the occupant of the nearest small bed in the ward and said, 'Shall we proceed?'

It was Saturday and a chill wind had not kept those who had known and respected Mark Osbourne from making the journey to the clifftop to pay their respects to the memory of a brave and fearless man.

Daniel searched the crowd for a sight of Darcey but had no luck, until the latest tram-load of spectators arrived and she was the first person to alight amongst them, which gladdened his heart, knowing that at least she understood his feelings regarding the lifeboat.

But when the service was over and he looked for her in vain amongst the crowd again, it became obvious that she had left, that nothing had changed between them. His sister came up to him and said, 'I thought I saw Darcey. Has she gone?'

'It would appear so,' he replied, and as Cordelia glanced at him questioningly he explained, 'We have a problem, the two of us. I've asked her to marry me, but she is too aware of the perils of the lifeboat to say yes, for a very good reason. Darcey lost her parents in disastrous circumstances when she was in her early teens and had to bring up her young brother on her own, so now she dreads having to do the same with any children we might have, if the same happened to me as it did to Dad.'

'That is so sad for both of you!' Cordelia exclaimed. 'A chance of happiness away from old sorrows being blighted by your pasts.'

'I'm waiting to see if the powers that be can produce someone suitable to take over from me on the lifeboat,' he said, 'but so far there's no news from those quarters, and in the meantime the two of us are keeping a low profile regarding our love life, such as it is, so I'd be obliged if you would say nothing to anyone about it for the time being, Cordelia.'

Back at the apartment, after her brief appearance at the dedication ceremony, Darcey was wishing that she hadn't been in such a hurry to leave the proceedings. But the occasion had been more than she could bear, with the reason for it such a close reminder of her dread of loss and loneliness, and with those thoughts still uppermost there was the rest of Saturday to face on her own.

As she was digesting that thought the doorbell rang and when she opened it, Daniel said gravely, 'Thanks for attending the dedication ceremony, Darcey. I can imagine what an ordeal it must have been, and have come to take you for a meal if you are agreeable, leaving our differences and despair to disappear for a while.'

She smiled. 'I would like that very much.'

'So get your coat and off we go to the place that you liked so much the first time, if I remember rightly,' he commented, and thought they were acting as if there wasn't a cloud in their sky when in truth it was full of them.

He left his car in the hospital car park and as they walked the short distance to the restaurant he said, 'Cordelia was asking after you. She was disappointed not to have had the chance for a chat.'

'Yes, I know,' Darcey said regretfully. 'That was my fault entirely. I'll get in touch during the week.'

Changing the subject, he said, 'Easter will soon be upon us. Have you made any plans so far, or are you on duty on the ward? Only we never did go out for a sail with the Young Sailors' Club after the Christmas mix-up of your working hours, did we? Or are references to such matters taboo?'

'No, of course not,' she told him, so aware of his nearness she wanted to reach out and hold him close. But she hadn't forgotten the time when she'd thrust him away as he'd taken the call from the lifeboat house to say he was needed and spoiled their wonderful moment of desire. Everything had changed since then and she knew he was trying to avoid any further upsets between them.

The restaurant was busy but a table was found for them and as they waited to be served, various people who had been at the lighthouse dedication service in the afternoon stopped by to say how appropriate a gesture it had been in memory of such a man, and when they had gone she said chokingly, 'You must be very proud of your father.'

'Yes, I am,' he agreed unsmilingly, 'but I'm not looking for any of that sort of thing for myself.' And when the food arrived at the table just then, he made no further comment and neither did she, but both were conscious of the moment that had come out of nowhere.

When the meal was over they walked slowly back to the apartment and on arriving Darcey said, 'Would you like to come in for a drink before you go?'

'Er...yes, that would be nice,' he said, aware of the message in the last three words of the invitation, but reluctant to miss the chance of spending more time with her. Inside her apartment, he couldn't help but glance through the open door of her bedroom as she hung up the winter coat that she'd been wearing, his gaze falling on the neat single bed that she slept in. With the thought of his luxurious double bed, which he so much wanted to share with her, and with the weight of the moment heavy upon him, he said, 'I think I'll give the drink a miss, if you don't mind. I've got a busy day in the operating theatre tomorrow.'

'Yes, of course,' she said flatly, and as he turned to go she added, 'The meal was lovely, Daniel. Thank you so much.'

'It was a pleasure, as is anything that we do together,' he replied, and with a brief goodbye quickly headed off into the night. When he'd returned to the silence of the empty rooms of his apartment he groaned inwardly, and once the door was locked he climbed the elegant staircase to the master bedroom and stood looking down at the bed that was so much more attractive than the neat, white-sheeted, single one he'd observed in Darcey's bedroom, which was still making his blood warm.

Would he ever have the joy of carrying her up here as his bride? he thought. There was a determination in her that came from her fear of loss and loneliness that he understood and wished he didn't, and with regard to finding another coxswain to replace him on the lifeboat, it was proving to be much harder than he had thought it would be, but there was no way he would ever leave the crew short in number. He had expected to have heard from the authorities before now with regard to his request for someone to replace him as when it eventually occurred it would leave him free to marry Darcey, which he longed to do, but there would always be the feeling of loss in his life that came from a lack of contact with the restless sea.

The last thing he did before settling for the night was to check whether her light was still on, and when he saw that the apartment was in darkness Daniel visualised her sleeping alone in the small white bed and his heart ached at the thought of the hurt he was causing her by wanting to hang onto his grim resolve.

For a long time Darcey had lain awake, wondering what would happen next, and how long they were going to continue the cat and mouse charade that they were playing out. With those thoughts running around her head, sleep had eluded her until at last she'd slept fitfully, though not for long, as the strident sound of her bedside alarm clock had soon brought her back to reality and the agenda of the day ahead.

With morning came a hint of spring. A pale sun shone in a cloudless sky and the sea was the calmest Darcey had seen since coming to Seahaven. Soon it would be Easter and Alexander would be here, she thought, and when he met him, Daniel would realise how special he was to her, the young brother that she had cared for, and maybe would understand how now she wanted children of her own with him, Daniel, as their father, but needed to know that he wouldn't be placing his life at risk.

It was Sunday and sometimes she was on duty on the children's ward, but not today. With that first glimpse of spring from the pale sun above she had the urge to be out and about, and as she was debating how and where, in the middle of the morning Cordelia rang to invite her to lunch if she was free.

'Yes, I am,' Darcey said. 'I would love to come. I owe you an apology for not seeking you out after the ceremony, Cordelia.'

'You don't owe me anything,' came the reply. 'The girls are looking forward to seeing you and so are Lawrence and I…and Daniel would be too if he knew you are joining us. But he has that pleasure to come when he arrives to have lunch with us, which is usually after his Sunday morning with the young sailors.' Into the silence that followed, Cordelia commented, 'But today he will be showing a possible applicant for his position on the lifeboat what sort of a set-up we have with our rescue facilities.'

'Yes, I see,' Darcey said, as light dawned that Daniel had been keeping to his side of the agreement that she'd demanded of him so forcibly, and now might be free of his commitment to the lifeboat service.

'I'm not so sure it will be as easy as that,' she told her flatly. 'The two of us aren't in agreement about the future because my past was a joyless thing once I lost my parents, with my young brother to care for and a living to earn, and if anything should happen to Daniel while on the lifeboat, I would be lost for evermore.'

'I understand how you feel as I worry too, but I should also say that it is rarely that a life or lives are lost under those conditions,' Cordelia said gently. 'However, obviously there is an element of risk that has to be accepted in the process, and if he does have to stay on the lifeboat crew, it will be for you to decide how much of that you can cope with on a long-term basis.'

'I've known that from the start,' she told her friend. 'I carry the thought around with me all the time, which is why I asked Daniel to be free of the perils of the lifeboat service when we marry, and he has agreed. But I am conscious of the strong ties he had with your father with regard to saving the lives of others as if what he does at Oceans House isn't enough.'

'Yes, maybe,' Cordelia agreed, 'but don't stay away from having lunch with us, Darcey. He will be disappointed to have missed you if you do.'

But not so upset that he had told her what he was going to be involved with during the morning, she thought tearfully. Yet she treasured her friendship with his sister, didn't want to upset her, and so she said, 'No, of course not. It will be lovely to see you all.'

When Daniel arrived at his sister's house just before lunchtime, he found Darcey swathed in bandages with the small would-be nurses in attendance. Laughter replaced the morning's traumas momentarily, but having spent most of it reluctantly showing another coxswain around his boat, with the thought of what it might mean in the long run, his amusement was short-lived.

'I called at your place earlier to let you know what I was going to be involved in during the morning, but there was no answer. Where were you?' he questioned.

'The spring sunshine had tempted me out and I'd gone for a stroll along the promenade,' she told him. 'When I got back Cordelia phoned and invited me to have lunch with you all.'

'So you already know where I've been?'

'Well, yes. Why didn't you tell me before?'

'Because I only got the message that this guy was coming a couple of hours before he was due.'

'And?' she breathed.

'He liked everything, except the fact that it would mean him having to move house, and he wasn't prepared to accept that.'

'And he's the only one?'

'Well, yes, of course! Do you think I've been holding them back to suit my own ends, Darcey? The answer to that is I am deeply committed to what I do now regarding the lifeboat service, but as there are very good reasons why I don't want to cause you pain or hurt I shall leave the service when the right moment presents itself. But under the current circumstances I think we should let things cool down for a while, don't you?'

'Whatever you say,' she said raggedly, and if Cordelia hadn't appeared at that moment to say that lunch was ready, she would have made her apologies and left after being made to feel so unwanted. But she cared for her friend too much to spoil the occasion and chatted mostly to the children while Daniel and Lawrence discussed sport and their hostess smiled at them all, unaware of the tense conversation earlier that had taken place between their guests.

As the sunny afternoon changed to gathering dusk Darcey explained to her friend that Alex was due to phone in the early evening regarding him visiting Seahaven in the near future, and said her farewells, but as she prepared to walk the short distance home, Daniel said, 'I'll take you in the car. It isn't a good time to be out on your own, before the streetlamps come on.'

'I'll be fine,' she said quietly, and for his ears alone added, 'I thought we were going to have a cooling-off time?'

'Yes, we are,' he agreed. 'But not at this moment.' He called to his sister, who had gone to fetch Darcey's coat from the cloakroom, 'I'm taking Darcey home and will be back shortly.'

Cordelia nodded with the thought in mind that she had longed for him to find someone to love and cherish and prayed that Darcey would be the one, but there were bridges to cross and long-ago hurts had to heal for both of them first. Only then would it come right.

CHAPTER TEN

NO WORDS PASSED between them until Daniel stopped the car outside the apartment and then he broke the silence to say, 'Give my regards to your brother, Darcey. Why don't you suggest to him that he come to live here? He could join the Young Sailors' Club.'

She smiled for the first time since they'd left his sister's house and told him, 'He is already having yearnings. Maybe his visit here over Easter will help him make that decision. But it would mean going to a different university in September.'

'Yes, of course,' he said thoughtfully as she bade him a brief goodbye, and as he drove back to his sister's house it seemed strange that he, Daniel, should have the kind of family that Darcey and her brother had never had due to losing their parents, and it had to be why she so longed for a marriage that was free of worry and loneliness.

If he could give her that there would be joy in the giving of it, but the gift of life that he had given to so many caught in the ocean's grip would have to be passed on to someone else and he was going to miss that.

But first a new coxswain had to be found, and until that was done there was going to be no change in the situation in which he found himself, and added to that Easter was drawing near, with lots of would-be sailors on the seas around Seahaven, thinking they had the upper hand and coming unstuck. Maybe the fates would be good and give him one last time to copy his father if his replacement still had to be found. But no way did he want anything that he might be called on to do to cause Darcey hurt or sorrow.

With regard to his love for Darcey, he had wanted her from the moment of their meeting, had known that she was the answer to years of emptiness after a dead marriage, and when she'd responded to his feelings with similar delight it had been fantastic, until her memories of the past and his involvement with the lifeboat had taken away the joy of their romance.

Back in the solitude of her apartment, Darcey was on the phone to Alex confirming the date of his Easter visit, which was going to commence in three weeks' time on the day before Good Friday until the middle of the following week, when he was planning to fly out to Bangkok to continue his travels.

'I'm really looking forward to being near the sea,' he said. 'There is a lake near here where some of us spend all our free time between shifts and it's great, but is nothing compared to the sea. I can't wait to see it. How often do you go sailing?'

'Never have so far,' she told him flatly, with the memory of the times that Daniel had wanted her to join him and the crew from the Young Sailors' Club and been unsuccessful. 'Maybe you'll be able to show me how.'

'Sure, it's easy-peasy,' he promised, and when the call was over and the usual silence fell over the apartment, the thought was there that the safest place where Alex could sail would be as a member of the Young Sailors' Club under Daniel's guidance, instead of wherever with an overdose of confidence.

The next morning Easter seemed far away. Mondays were always busy after the weekend when young members of the population had been out and about and been less than careful during their weekend activities, which had brought them to Oceans House.

As Darcey and Daniel did the rounds of the children's ward there was little time for any other matters than the health of their young patients, and it wasn't until he was done and ready to move upwards to where the older folk awaited him that he asked, 'Are you all right after yesterday's twists and turns?'

'Yes, I suppose so,' she said. 'I ask too much of you and I'm sorry, Daniel.'

'Don't be,' he chided gently. 'Just be yourself.' Then he was gone, leaving her to question what his real feelings were.

* * *

The days were getting longer and lighter. The sun no longer preferred to hide behind cloud so much, but still there was no one to replace him, Daniel thought. It was a situation that the rest of the lifeboat crew were totally happy with, and probably also with those who trained and staffed the boats, from the look of things, as no changes of crew were being considered, which left only Darcey with any reservations regarding the situation. He braced himself for the day that had to come sooner or later, but which was a long time in coming.

At last on the following Sunday morning Daniel took Darcey sailing in the boat that had been a wreck the first time she'd seen it, and was now back to its normal performance with a full crew of trainee mariners on board, along with themselves and Ely, and she thought that Alex, when he came in two weeks' time, would enjoy this sort of thing, with others of a similar age. They sailed closer to home than the lifeboat due to their youth, but were just as welcome when needed.

When they arrived back at their headquarters next to the harbour, Bridget provided lunch, after which the group would hold their weekly meeting with Daniel in charge. Darcey was aware of how much the young folk owed him for the time and patience he had for them, which was bettered only by his devotion to saving the lives of those who might lose them without him and others like him.

He was watching her expression and as their eyes met it was there again, the feeling of rightness that was all wrong when she tried to be sensible. On that thought she thanked him for taking her out in the sailing club's boat and went back to what was left of another free Sunday, which was an event, and would have to be made up for soon.

Daniel stared after her, wishing that she hadn't been in such a hurry so that he could have taken her somewhere after the meeting for a few moments on their own. But maybe Darcey wanted to avoid that sort of thing with their relationship up in the air and each of them having their own kind of longings.

In the days that followed, Darcey marked each one on the calendar as Easter drew nearer and with it Alex's arrival in Seahaven, and always was the thought that just for once she would have someone of her own to be with for a short time of togetherness, as her love for Daniel had become a cloistered thing due to the circumstances of it, but the need was still there.

Her brother's arrival was due to take place at midday on Thursday, and Darcey thought glumly that she wasn't going to be around to meet him until the evening as she was on duty for most of that day. So much for the two Sundays of free time that she'd just had. But it didn't seem to worry Alex much when she phoned to tell him.

'No problem,' he said airily when she told him.

'Once I've taken my gear to the place where you've booked me to stay I'll find plenty to do. Just looking at the sea will be great. I'll be waiting for you outside the hospital when you come out in the evening, and then we'll live it up, eh, sis?'

'Er…yes,' she said laughingly. 'Am I going to be allowed time to change out of my uniform?'

'Sure,' was the reply.

She hadn't seen much of Daniel socially since he'd taken her sailing with the young people in their boat. It was as if he was avoiding her but he'd also mentioned he was looking forward to meeting her brother, or so he'd said, which she supposed was better than nothing, and perhaps she could take the two of them out to dinner one night.

'Yes, maybe,' he agreed when she suggested it, with the thought in his mind that chance might be a fine thing if the lifeboat was called out as often as it usually was at such times.

At the end of her working day on the Thursday there was no Alex waiting to greet her, and as her apartment was only feet away Darcey hurried home, but he wasn't waiting there either, and when she tried to phone him there was no answer.

Yet she knew that he had arrived safely that afternoon because he'd rung her to say that he'd settled himself into the small flatlet on the seafront that she'd found for him and was going to spend the rest of the afternoon down by the sea until she'd finished work, so where was he?

Hopefully it was just bad timing and she walked on to the seafront and looked around her from there. She saw a crowd gathered to watch something that was causing much interest and her heart skipped a beat. The lifeboat had been called out and was speeding in the direction of the far end of the bay in what was one of the roughest seas for some time. She could just see the form of a young guy at the mercy of a rough sea, being swept up against rocks and then thrown back into the water helpless against its force, and she froze with fear.

The lifeboat had just reached him and she saw Daniel and another of the crew go over the side with lifebelts. They pulled the seemingly lifeless body out of the water and she just knew it was Alex who was going to be taken from her this time as anguish turned her bones to chalk.

But they had him, one on each side, before the next onslaught of the sea came back upon them, and as Daniel and the crew worked on their charge, the lifeboat ploughed its way back to safety amid cheers from those who had watched, while Darcey ran frantically to where it had been launched to await its return.

Bridget was there and on seeing her said, 'They've radioed from the boat that he's unconscious. Don't know who the lad is, but he can't have a better chance than with our team. They'll be here any moment and he will be taken straight to Oceans House where Daniel will examine him, and if he needs further treatment he'll be taken to the hospital in the town centre.'

'He's my brother,' she said chokingly, 'and is all I have in the world. But in just a matter of moments it doesn't feel like that any more.'

'It's here, the boat. You'll be able to see him in a moment and go with him to hospital,' Bridget said consolingly. 'There's an ambulance waiting to take him to Oceans House with Daniel on board, which is the usual procedure on this sort of occasion, and if you ask he'll take you with him.'

Darcey didn't hear her last comment. Her fears were confirmed as she watched the crew stretchering Alex off the boat with Daniel supervising, and when he saw her he said raggedly, 'When I saw him close to I was horrified. I couldn't believe it, you are so alike, and I knew that he was coming to stay.'

'Is he going to live, Daniel?' she croaked, as she looked down at her brother's still form.

'Yes, if it is anything to do with me,' he gritted. 'He's breathing more levelly now and I've given you enough worry and heartache. Hopefully there won't be any more once we get Alex to Oceans House.' He nodded at a signal from the ambulance driver. 'In you get. It will be just a matter of minutes before we're on home ground.'

At that moment Alex opened his eyes for a fleeting second and mumbled, 'What have I done, Darcey?'

'Fought the spring tide and lost,' she told him, 'and Dr Osbourne and I are taking you to Oceans House to be sorted out.'

'Sounds good,' was his only comment before he drifted back into semi-consciousness.

Daniel said, 'We need to go straight into X-Ray when we arrive and deal with it from there. I am so sorry this has happened to your brother, Darcey. It must have heightened your fear of lifeboats even more.'

She managed a smile. 'That isn't so, Daniel. It has made me realise how fortunate are they who are served by the lifeboat in their hour of need. I'd got it all wrong, and I don't want you to change anything regarding what you do. Without you and your team out there, Alex would have died.'

The ambulance was pulling into its parking space at Oceans House and as her young brother was carried carefully inside and straight to X-Ray, with Daniel and herself in attendance, Alex regained consciousness again and said, 'I was playing a game, dodging the big waves when they came, but they got too fast for me, and now am I going to have to spend Easter in hospital?'

'It all depends on how much you have hurt yourself,' Daniel told him. 'The X-rays are going to tell us that, and in future remember that the sea isn't always a friend, far from it.'

The results they were waiting for after a session in X-Ray were a mixture of good and not so good, as Darcey observed them issuing forth in the form of a fractured arm and massive bodily bruising in most areas. But both she and Daniel were aware that it could have been much worse, and when Alex asked what it all meant he listened in silence to what they had to say and then asked again if it was going to mean him being kept in the hospital for a while and couldn't he stay with Darcey until he was well again?

'Her accommodation isn't big enough for someone else to stay with her,' Daniel told him, 'neither would it be allowed, and it would not be wise for you to continue staying alone in your flat on the promenade until you are well again, but I do have a suggestion.

'How would you like to come and stay with me? I have a spare bedroom, so would be able to keep an eye on you during the night, and bring you with me for the day each morning where you could get better by resting and watching your sister and myself performing our daily tasks.'

'Wow!' Alex said weakly. 'That would be great!' His gaze went to Darcey, who had stood by speechless as Daniel got to know his prospective young brother-in-law. 'What about that, sis?'

'Yes, what about it,' she replied, smiling through her tears, and she turned to Daniel. 'He can stay here tonight while we sort out our arrangements for the future, don't you think?' she asked him.

'Absolutely,' he said. 'But first let's get that arm set and put in a cast.'

Once that had been accomplished, Alex was taken

to the men's ward and Daniel and Darcey made sure that he was safely settled with all details of his injuries given to staff for that night.

Then they left him in hospital care with an arrangement that they would call back soon, and went to Daniel's apartment where he showed her the guest room that would be occupied by her brother for as long as he needed it, and then took her into the main bedroom. As Darcey gazed at the empty bed he said gently, 'There has always been a place for you beside me, still is for that matter, but the ideal time for a beginning would be on our wedding night in the manor house, don't you think, with the vows we have made like stars in a cloudless sky. Will you marry me, Darcey?'

'Yes,' she said. 'I understand everything better now. As I watched you save Alex's life it was as if a blindfold had been removed from my eyes.'

'So where do you want to live when we become as one?' he said gently, and was surprised at the reply when it came.

'In the manor house near where you have preserved your father's memory for all time,' she said softly, and he observed her in amazement.

'You want to live in the place where you spent hours in the dark and the cold!'

'Yes, I'm afraid so,' she said with a smile, 'because it brought you to me, and we can make it lovely, Daniel. Also maybe sometime Cordelia and Lawrence might decide to join us in one of the other houses, or Alex could be a regular visitor once it has been brought to life again. We can make it beautiful and once we are settled there we can turn the rest of the village into a place that our children and those of others will love to live in.'

'Either of those things would be fantastic,' he said gently, holding her close, 'but first I want you to myself for a while. So before we go back to check on our young patient, can we fix on a date for a wedding and decide which local firm is going to be given the task of transforming our future habitation?'

'Yes, please,' she said, starry-eyed, and he kissed her long and lingeringly before they retraced their steps to Oceans House to check on Alexander, who was now sleeping after his frightening experience of earlier.

EPILOGUE

It was Christmas again in Seahaven and snow was gently falling as an event was taking place not far from the refurbished lighthouse and the now elegant manor house, where a twinkling Christmas tree was already in place to welcome the bride and groom, who would be returning for a wedding breakfast, along with their friends and relations after the ceremony in the village church.

Cordelia, the bridegroom's sister, was hostess for the event and delighted to be so, while her husband Lawrence was to give the bride away, and Alex, on top form, was greeting friends and neighbours as they arrived for the service in the small church, which was decorated with holly and ivy for Christmas and which hadn't seen a wedding in a long time. When Daniel heard the music change to welcome the bride he turned slowly and she was there with her eyes sparkling and mouth tender, his beautiful Christmas bride in a long white gown carrying a bouquet of red roses, and his heart sang with joy.

* * * * *